The Atlantis Girl

Book 1

The Atlantis Saga

S.A. Beck

ISBN-13: 978-1987859096
ISBN-10: 198785909X

Contents

Prologue

JANUARY 4, 2016, UTAH DATA
CENTER

8:15 AM

In the foothills of Utah was a group of squat white buildings isolated from the community at large. It was a place where data was mined, part of a global network run by the United States National Security Agency.

Data mining was big business, and there was money in it, but more important, it saved lives. How better to hear of threats to national security than from the terrorists themselves? The NSA was the branch of American government busy minding other people's business, but there was more to the department than met the eye. In a corner of one of the bland block buildings was the Department of Paranormal Threat Monitoring led by Gerard Terrace.

He was in charge of a particular sector of data mining that had little to do with weapons and revolutionaries. Gerard was in charge of a much more secret sector—the supernatural.

A no-nonsense man, Gerard was not the kind to believe every cockamamie story about telekinesis and people walking on water, but it wasn't his job to believe. It was his job to report. It was someone else's job to verify and someone else's job to sort the frivolous from the factual, and he was glad neither of those was his job, because he was good at reporting.

The balding middle-aged man accessed the building by security code and took the shiny chrome elevator up to his floor. He remembered what it had been like to work a normal civilian job in New York, how conversations would be buzzing through the halls in the mornings—the water cooler talk. The military wasn't like that. Most of the other employees lived in constant suspicion and surveillance of one another. It was their job.

Scrutinizing keywords in phone conversations, video recordings, computer chats—snooping, digging, decoding—it was what they did. Gerard heaved a sigh as he passed another closed face and barely mumbled good morning on the way to his office. He was being unkind, he knew, to think of them all as suspicious beetles scurrying to their respective holes. His subordinates were probably in a tizzy because an important visitor was coming to the facility, and no one wanted to appear out of line.

"General Hector Meade," Gerard mumbled to himself, keying in the code to his door and entering his orderly domain. A black oak desk dominated the spacious interior, which had only two other chairs besides his. The walls, cheerless and bland, were paneled in an expensive wood grain that gleamed under the light. The floors gleamed, too—black marble with blue veins. His office was studiously minimalist and to his tastes. Gerard couldn't stand excess.

He smiled in pleasure at the parallel walls of black-tinted windows overlooking the marvelous desert. His office was at the top of the building, prime company real estate. Gerard hadn't always had the top spot. He had started much like the others on the floor. He was in charge merely because of being inordinately good at seeing through the nonsense to the necessary. Gerard was an expert intelligence analyst, and he was about to prove yet again how invaluable he was to the service of his country.

Gerard was meeting with the general and several other higher-ups for a presentation on the data he had compiled on elite civilians worthy of closer scrutiny, possibly for military or Secret Service recruit. People like Stanton Walden of Indiana, the boy with the high IQ and ability to learn foreign languages after only brief exposure to them. Gerard had plenty of people like that on his list.

He had spent years on the pet project that had yielded a sizable database of reported supernaturals, data verified by others, sorted, and sent back to him. His people had scoured the sea of incoming information like large nets fishing for small minnows. People like Walden weren't easy to find. Their unbelievable abilities usually weren't mentioned except on hoax or conspiracy websites and in passing conversations, but Gerard had found them because he had listened when others had scoffed.

Few had been aware of his purposes for compiling the list, but now everyone would know—everyone who was anyone with the security credentials to know. Gerard rubbed his hands together in avid anticipation as he sat down in his comfortable black chair and prepared his notes.

For all his listening ears and watchful eyes, Gerard had no idea that while he was waiting for the important meeting scheduled for later in the evening, General Meade was on his way across the country to pick up a woman with a similar agenda, Dr. Akiko Yamazaki of Arizona State University. She wasn't military or government affiliated. She was probably closer to anti-establishment.

She was a world-renowned anthropologic geneticist, and she specialized in ancient civilizations and their descendants. If anyone could benefit from Gerard's list, it was the woman with the scientific know-how to trace the origins of the subjects' special capabilities and find a genetic component for their differences from other human populations.

Simply put, Akiko could tell General Meade and his associates what made the supernaturals super.

While Gerard was gathering his notes, Akiko was climbing the steps of the stage in her arena-style classroom, crossing to the podium, and staring down at her small feet as she walked. She was lost in thought, trying to figure out how to get her project from planning phase to research phase with classes to teach and college students to settle down and instruct. She sighed at having her real work interrupted for the tedious tasks, but she pushed her half-glasses up the bridge of her nose and set her laptop computer on the podium to get started.

"Good morning, class."

The mic's feedback made the students clutch their ears and groan en masse. Akiko softly apologized in accented English, fiddling with the device to turn it down or off. She had almost figured out the mic controls when the double doors to the classroom burst open, admitting two broad-shouldered gentlemen with forgettable faces and similar medium brown hair. They wore identical black suits and identical opaque sunglasses, and had identical official-looking strides. Akiko backed away in surprise as they swiftly crossed the room.

"Y-yes? May I help you?" she stammered. As one of the men stoically gripped her above the elbows and ushered her toward the door, she said, "What on earth are you doing?"

"Dr. Yamazaki, please remain calm. We need you to come with us," he murmured with dictatorial firmness. "Everything will be explained to you shortly." The doctor didn't resist. She knew what happened to people who resisted authority, and the men appeared to have an authority she lacked.

As she was removed from the stage, Akiko heard the buzz of conversation erupt from her alarmed students, everyone wondering what was going on. Akiko looked back, noting several people recording the scene with their cell phones. At least someone would be left to tell the tale. "This has to be some kind of a joke," she grumbled, not amused.

The other gentleman stepped to the podium and addressed the arena. "The dean of Life Sciences would like to extend his apologies for the interruption of your course; however, Dr. Yamazaki's class will resume next week, as scheduled. Please remain seated until you receive email confirmation you are allowed to leave."

"What?" Akiko shook her head to negate the claim, but students happy to ditch class overlooked the gesture. The two men half led and half dragged her out the doors, shuffling her across the bright, sunny campus to a black sedan parked curbside. Akiko's heart began to race. The men in black suits might be able to convince gullible undergraduates that they were school-sanctioned, but the professor knew better. The dean hadn't contacted her. Who were those men?

"No, no. You're not taking me anywhere!" she protested, balking at being forced into the car. The men released her and stood with hands clasped behind their backs. A man in military uniform stepped from the sedan.

She didn't recognize him, but he seemed to be the man in charge. Maybe he could tell her what was going on. "Who are these people, and why have you forced me from my class? Do you even have permission to be here? Wait until the university hears about this."

General Hector Meade, placating her, held up his hands and smiled. "Dr. Yamazaki, allow me to apologize on behalf of my personal staff. They can be... overbearing. I'm sorry about that, ma'am." His voice was a rich baritone, his tone conciliatory. Akiko's angry tirade died on her lips. General Meade continued, "I'm here regarding your recent application for grant funding for a special research project, DNA of extinct civilizations, to let you know that the application will gladly be funded. I'm also here because we'd like you to work closely with us. You see, your expertise is exactly what we're looking for to help with a project of our own."

Akiko frowned, wondering why the military would be interested in her work. Her current research project was a search for telltale DNA traces of a particular lost civilization. Not many in the scientific community were aware of exactly what she was after, and there was no reason for those outside the scientific community to know.

"You could've sent a correspondence," she said, suspicious of the smooth-talking general. She had worked on projects with official US departments before, and things were decidedly off protocol.

He chuckled, a raspy sound. "I'd like you to be part of a meeting later today where a thorough list of test participants has been assembled. Everything else—details of the work you'll be doing for us—will be outlined there. Of course, you don't have to go. But"—he leaned toward her with a wink—"this is a once-in-a-lifetime opportunity. Your research contributions will literally change the entire world as we know it. Are you up for that? Or would you rather go back in there and watch kids fall asleep to your lectures? Your choice."

The professor kept her expression blank, revealing nothing of her thoughts. Test participants were precisely what she needed but only those with certain characteristics. "What sort of list?" she asked. She didn't want to seem too interested. Then again, Akiko wondered if the grant funding hinged upon her accepting the military job offer. If that was the case, she really didn't have a choice.

"Take a ride with me, Doctor. You want to see this list for yourself. My description won't do it justice. But I promise... you won't regret this one."

Chapter 1

MARCH 1, 2016, SAN FRANCISCO, CALIFORNIA

9:00 AM

The teenage girl with the arctic blue eyes, still as glacial lakes, sat in the near-empty courtroom listening to the judge dryly deliver her sentence. Judge Katherine Colby glowered from her podium, the cherry wood dais a throne overlooking the two tables at opposite sides of the room. At one of them sat Jaxon and her counsel. Behind Jax was a partition separating the main floor from the empty pews. It was disheartening to be backed by no one.

Jaxon Ares Andersen had heavy-lidded, almond-shaped eyes with an Asian tilt, and her honey-hued brown face never strayed from sullen disinterest despite the gravity of the situation. Her lustrous jet-black hair fell in ripples to the collar of the navy-blue dress her caseworker had insisted she wear, though it was a size too big, and Jaxon looked like a child playing dress-up. She was skinny and underdeveloped, and she would have appeared closer to thirteen or fourteen than her actual age were it not for her ice-blue eyes, which looked far older and worldlier as she scanned the place.

She was familiar with the courtroom. The diminutive teen had once been terrified when squaring off with the legal system, but she no longer cared what any of the "systems" wanted to do with her. As a foster kid, she was aware systems failed girls like her on a daily basis.

She had been nine months old when she became a ward of the state, and she had often imagined there had to be something from her past—from "before"—that teased at the fringes of her memory, but the only life Jax had ever known was one of transitions. Despite the ease with which other infants and toddlers were adopted or placed in foster homes, little Jaxon had remained unclaimed until she was four years old and, finally, someone opted to give her a try.

By the time she was five, she was kicked out again after getting into a fight with the much older biological son of her foster mom after he punched Jax in the face. Jaxon had easily overpowered him and sprained his ankle in the process. At sixteen, she found that the bullying from her younger days seemed to get worse with each passing year. She had only gotten older, stronger, and less willing to put up with other people's crap... and more liable to get into trouble for simply defending herself.

Sighing in frustration, Jax sat still at the table, a complex exercise of slowing her racing thoughts and controlling her normal restlessness. There was nothing she could do about the tapping of her foot. It wouldn't stop. She gripped the tabletop with fingers sporting chipped black nail polish, her translucent eyes skittering around the room at every distraction—the flickering bulb of a light soon to blow, an errant fly drowsily floating above the judge's head. The quiet coughs and rustling of her public defender and social worker overshadowed the monotonous voice droning on about her charges.

Truancy, juvenile delinquency, assault and battery—she had a serious rap sheet.

Jaxon sighed and tried to focus on what Judge Colby was saying. "… Benevolent prosecutor recommends placement in a more structured environment, as it is evident the juvenile has not previously benefited from close supervision and structure, and so I have taken his recommendations into consideration, along with the extensive records of Mrs. Jenkins detailing extenuating circumstances surrounding the defendant's behavior."

Jaxon was intrigued by the lines in the old magistrate's face. She could count the multitude of grays in the woman's hair. Jax knew the middle-aged blonde controlled her future, but she wanted to at least appear involved in the decision-making process. *How unruly could she be?* she wondered. After all, there were appearances to keep up. Everyone expected Jaxon to be on her worst behavior.

"The juvenile's past record and age also played a part in my deliberation, as I believe the defendant is mature enough to perfectly understand the gravity of her actions. Therefore, I cannot, in good conscience, approve of using the defendant's previous history of abuses or any negligence on the part of her foster parents as the sole excuses for her delinquency. Ms. Andersen, in my twenty years in this job, I've seen minors in far worse situations than yours make better decisions and choose to straighten out their lives. I'm one of them. So I'm sorry, but you have no excuse."

Jaxon snorted loudly and crossed her arms over her meager chest, but the judge barely flinched at the irreverence, lifted a slender brow, and carried on.

"For the reasons outlined above, it is the opinion of this court that the defendant, Jaxon Andersen, would most benefit from placement in a group home for a duration of two years until she reaches maturity." Jaxon should have been relieved she wasn't being carted off to juvenile detention, but she wasn't. She was on guard, well aware that anywhere she was sent would offer the same challenges as the places before.

There would always be someone looking to take advantage of her, rob her, and lie about her. There would still be fistfights and bruised egos. With a shake of her head and a swish of her glossy black shoulder-length hair, she muttered, "Well, let's see what the group home has in store."

"Shh!" her social worker hissed.

Jaxon squeezed the table in frustration and felt the wood take on the imprint of her fingertips beneath her impossibly strong grip. She must have imagined it. She discreetly lifted her hand, and the round whirls and ridges of her fingers were tattooed into the wood. "What the...?" Jaxon quickly and quietly slid a folder over the three fingerprints, pretending nothing had happened. The scarred wood had to have always borne the indentions. She didn't want to get blamed for vandalism, too. Jaxon sighed in irritation.

The judge continued, "If the defendant fails to adhere to the rulings of this court, the defendant will be required to perform community service for a duration of 242 hours in conjunction with a period of probation to last no less than two years. Court is adjourned."

The gavel dropped. The years of bouncing from foster home to foster home were over, but Jaxon knew there was nowhere she could go where she wouldn't face a struggle. Fortunately, nothing lasted forever. She had been in nearly every type of home, each placement lasting no more than two or three years. A time or two, Jax had even thought she'd struck gold with a family only to be returned to the foster care system. She concluded that some people were too different to fit in with normal society, and maybe she was one of them.

But as she glanced at the marks in the scarred wood of the table, she gritted her teeth resolutely, lifting her chin and squaring her shoulders. There was no point being fatalistic. She might finally find her place in the world or she might not, but whatever she faced next, she would endure. She was stronger than anyone gave her credit for being.

MARCH 14, 2016, SAN FRANCISCO, CALIFORNIA

10:30 AM

Her clunky smartphone was safely tucked against her chest, and Jaxon rested her head on the cool glass window of her caseworker's Elantra. They were driving at a sedate pace to Jaxon's new prison, also known as the Forever Welcome Group Home for Juveniles. Helen Jenkins had scored Jax the cushy deal that landed her in the less restrictive facility, as Judge Colby certainly hadn't been in a generous mood. Jaxon was grateful, but she was still anxious about getting there.

She gnawed on her bottom lip and glanced at Helen, one of the few constants in her life. Jax had been stuck with the same caseworker for years. The woman's frizzy red hair framed a round, dimpled face. Helen had kind, concerned gray eyes, more often than not filled with disappointment when looking at Jax, and she had a matronly air. She was the closest thing to a mother that Jax had, but Helen wasn't her mom. She was the poor, unfortunate fool who'd gotten stuck handling Jaxon's mishaps.

"It's really not that bad," said Helen. "I've had kids placed in group homes before who end up loving the place." She gripped the steering wheel and smiled as she stared straight ahead, ignoring Jaxon's eye roll.

"That's what you always say, Hels."

"You should probably *try* a little harder to love it this time, Jax. I mean, c'mon. How many homes can you get kicked out of, huh? The Ramses were nice enough people. I can't believe you didn't work out with that family. What was so bad about Preston High that you had to fight your way to expulsion? Tell me that."

Jaxon rolled her eyes again, unwilling to talk about the fights she'd had at school while placed with the Ramses. Friendly, jovial Helen wouldn't understand. Jax had always been the runt of the litter, the easiest person to pick on. She was barely five feet tall and petite, and while Jax didn't consider herself much of a looker, apparently other girls at her former school considered her enough of a threat to make her life miserable.

Jax was a fighter. She always had been and probably always would be. She sighed. "Maybe they should try a little harder to love me this time, Helen."

Helen cleared her throat uneasily, wordlessly agreeing with Jaxon, and deflected the conversation with small talk Jaxon wasn't in the mood to hear. Jax grumbled affirmations every few minutes while she zoned out to the music coming through earbuds attached to her smartphone, the guitars screaming and bass pounding in her eardrums.

She bit her nails as she stared out the window at the San Francisco landscape zipping past. The warm leather seat beneath her thighs and the hum of the tires against the pavement had a lulling effect, and she fought sleep. As Helen drove out of the suburbs, her gradual acceleration reminded Jaxon she was again running from one instability to another. That was the way it felt every time she had to move.

It was bittersweet not to belong to anyone, to hope against hope that something about herself might attract a mother or father. It was much like making a love connection—probably the ultimate love connection. Jax had given up hope of ever having real parents, but she was ready to at least have a life of her own.

Jax snuggled up in the seat with her feet tucked under her body and her face to the sunny window, and Helen finally left her alone. Jaxon had things to think. Her mind was a crowded playground of ideas.

The miles ticked away beneath her as she dozed, until sometime later, Jaxon stretched and looked around. The tinny sound of music came from the earbuds that had fallen out of her ears. "Damn, we're not there yet?" She had fallen asleep and lost track of time. She couldn't tell whether they had been traveling for minutes or hours, but the scenery was changing.

"Watch your language," Helen muttered. The car accelerated and zoomed farther away from the suburban San Francisco Bay area, and the terrain became hilly. The white Hyundai Elantra turned off the main highway and kicked up a spray of gravel as it traveled down what looked like a forgotten road. The gray ribbon of asphalt curved and wound its way deeper and deeper into a world Jaxon found unfamiliar.

With no car in sight for miles, it was as if she and Helen were the only people remaining. The landscape grew lusher, with vibrant green hills and, in the distance, dense, darker green forests. There was something enchanting about the place that made Jaxon perk up and peer out the window.

Helen took note and flashed an encouraging half smile in her direction. "Not much farther," she promised. "You'll like it out here in the country. It's peaceful, quiet. Look at the sky. Have you ever seen a blue so crystal clear?"

Jaxon tamped down her excitement at what she was seeing and slouched down in her seat, but the view beyond the window was unlike any she had ever seen, and she found herself sitting forward again after less than a mile. She was city born and city raised—in one household or another—and had never been farther than the suburbs. Snowy clouds shadowed vast fields of green. It seemed a lonesome place, sparsely populated, and it was easy to imagine that instead of traveling to some group home, they were going back in time to an era before humans existed.

After another turn and more miles of green ground and blue sky, the Elantra came upon a sprawling estate nestled in the valley of three hills. The manicured lawn stretched for acres and was enclosed by a brick and wrought-iron fence. Seeing the place—and knowing that she was arriving at her final destination before the foster system kicked her out into the real world—made Jaxon's heart pound harder and faster in her bony rib cage. The front gate opened slowly as Helen's car pulled up, and a sign read Forever Welcome. The house was a massive mansion, two stories high with gabled rooftops and an impressive entrance.

"This is it. Are you ready to start over?" Her social worker's voice was light, as if Helen already knew the answer.

"I'm always ready, Hels," said Jaxon. "My life is a book of do-overs." Jaxon squared her shoulders and lifted her chin. Helen's hands tightened on the wheel, and she kept her troubled eyes pointed ahead. She sighed and shook her head, and Jaxon shrugged.

"I hate to be the bearer of bad news, but I don't think you get any more second chances after this one. You've amassed quite a record between going to truancy court, the fights, and the squabbles with your foster parents. I had hoped you would—no—I know you have all the qualities people are looking for in a foster child, but it's time you stop blaming others and take ownership for bad behavior. You're not exactly Judge Colby's favorite person, and frankly, my supervisor has been at my neck about devoting more of my time to your case than any of my others."

"Typical," Jax muttered.

"I say all that to say, I can't come to your rescue anymore. The buck really stops here. If you can't make it at this group home, I'm afraid you're on your own."

Jaxon's eyes rose up and up to the top of the building and swept back down to the front door. The place wasn't what she had expected. Limestone bricks walled the ground level, and stucco in a Tudor architectural design covered the second story. A balcony extended above large double doors, and windows seemed to stare at the car as it cruised into the circular drive and eased to a halt at the front steps.

Jaxon took a deep breath and pushed her smartphone into her pocket, knowing places like the group home liked to confiscate things that didn't belong to them. She girded herself in the bravado she was known for—small and fierce—as the long-suffering Helen climbed out of the car with a grunt and sigh. The social worker stretched her stodgy body and trudged to the back of the car. The trunk popped open. Helen was saying something, but Jaxon wasn't paying her any attention.

She was overwhelmed by the new environment and scoping out the place. From the front seat of the car, she stared at the house. A rounded picture window took up the wall to the left of the front door, and she could see inside the house through the clear, dark glass. No busted-up furniture or scowling housemates were in sight. Her past experiences with welcomes made her wary of first days in a new place. Generally, there were cheery, bright falsities with undercurrents of the trouble to come. To find that no one was waiting at the window to greet her was...

different. Jax didn't know whether she should be grateful for the lack of fanfare or be even more on guard.

"Did you hear me, Jax?"

"What's up?"

"Come help me get your bags, girlie. They're waiting to meet you."

Jax frowned, climbing slowly out of the car and sneaking glances at the house over her shoulder as she ambled to the trunk to grab her suitcase. It wasn't as if she had a lot to carry inside. Helen marched ahead of her with the large Rubbermaid container holding the rest of her earthly possessions and rang the doorbell.

Jaxon waited at Helen's side and, when the door opened, felt a twinge of satisfaction upon seeing the stern-faced woman who answered. *At least something fits the stereotype,* she thought with a smirk. The woman had lank brown hair around a squat, boorish face, and she was dressed in a gray housedress that looked as if it had been pulled out of a closet from the 1950s.

"Yes? What is it?" she growled.

"Um, I'm Helen Jenkins, social worker for Jaxon Andersen," Helen said. The woman glared down at Jaxon and back at Helen. "I was told you were expecting us? I'm sure I have the right address. Forever Welcome, right?" The irony didn't escape Jaxon, who snickered behind her hand. The woman at the door was hardly welcoming. "I spoke with Dr. Hollis a few hours ago," Helen said.

Suddenly, another face appeared behind the scowler, and Helen stood up straighter to address the person beyond the woman. The man pushed forward with a friendly smile. "I'm Dr. Hollis, Ms. Jenkins—I'll handle this, Faye—Come in. Come right in. Jaxon? Pleasure to meet you." He wore an olive-colored tweed sweater, and glasses perched on the edge of his sharp nose. Waves of dark brown hair fell around his ears, and his smile was tucked in a thick beard. After shaking Helen's hand, he reached out to shake Jaxon's, but she hung back.

His warm smile didn't waver. Dr. Hollis stepped out of the way and ushered his guests inside. Helen and Jax stepped from the humid heat into the cool interior. The entryway to Forever Welcome, in keeping with a group home, had a large oak cubbyhole by the door with brass nameplates above each square. Knapsacks, purses, outer garments, and other belongings filled the spaces, and Jax surreptitiously perused the names as Helen and the doctor conversed.

Helen placed the Rubbermaid container by the door, and Dr. Hollis called a staff member in a gray uniform to carry the box away. Jax followed him with her eyes, idly wondering if any of her belongings would come up missing. But Forever Welcome didn't seem that sinister. Jax watched the original greeter march quietly down the hall and around a corner, thinking that perhaps she, too, was a staff member. Jax shrugged, putting aside her paranoia, and went back to looking around.

The walls of the entryway were a buff color, and the hardwood floor was covered in a dark red runner. The door was paneled with stained glass, its light washing the narrow space in sunny radiance. Along the opposite wall from the cubby was a bulletin board tacked with artwork and awards, and farther along the wall was a grouping of photographs. Jaxon set down her suitcase and slipped closer to look at the pictures.

"...Exactly as we discussed," she overheard Helen saying. "She has had some trouble in the past with bullies, and it puts her on the defensive. Occasionally, she'll lash out at imagined insults. Basically, any volatile situations should be avoided, so if you have anyone else with a fiery temperament, best to keep them separated."

"Ach, well, we're used to different personalities here at Welcome, Ms. Jenkins. I assure you our methods of treatment are sound." The doctor sounded casual and self-assured, in marked contrast to Helen's cautiousness and uncertainty.

"It was just a suggestion." Helen bristled. Jaxon glanced at the adults and noticed the doctor's placating smile, hand placed on the caseworker's arm. Jax sighed and turned back to the photos, faces of young people who had come in and out of the group home over the years. She reached up to touch a picture of a young boy with a dog. Jaxon pulled back her hand and turned away, disheartened. Her picture might go up on that wall, but she didn't belong there. She didn't belong anywhere.

"Oh no, no, not to imply your suggestion is unwarranted, Ms. Jenkins. Not at all. It's just to say I will personally do thorough testing and assign Ms. Andersen to the proper placement based on her results. But I appreciate your concern. As ever, your insight is invaluable."

"Thank you," Helen murmured, mollified. She blushed at the handsome psychiatrist and grinned girlishly until Jaxon materialized at her side with a bored glance at both of them.

"Right, so where's my room?"

Dr. Hollis graciously gestured for the pair to follow him. Jaxon grimaced at the prospect of losing her only tenuous hold on the familiar. She waved nervously to Helen and followed Dr. Hollis past the great room she had seen from outside to the flight of stairs at the end of the corridor.

"Ms. Jenkins, if you can wait for me here in my office"—he stopped in front of an open archway to the left of the staircase and looked in on what appeared to be a study nook—"I'll run Jaxon up to her new room and get back with you to do the paperwork. The director of the facility, Mr. Vance, will be joining us. This won't take but a minute."

"Of course. Of course."

Dr. Hollis lugged Jaxon's suitcase as she marched behind, and his bouncy brown hair fluttered around his face as he huffed and puffed his way up the lengthy flight. Jaxon looked down over the edge of the railing, trying to see what she hadn't been able to view from the entryway.

"You'll get a tour in a bit, Jaxon," Dr. Hollis promised, as if reading her mind.

She looked up at him, startled, noting his clear brown eyes and ready smile. "It's a little different than what I thought it would be."

"Most people have the wrong impression about group homes," he said. "But you're right. It's nothing like the norm. Here at Forever Welcome, we're a private-run facility supplemented by government grants, and we offer a unique program for troubled youth. Our residents receive homeschooling and career preparedness courses as well as counseling and guidance to help get them ready for life beyond these walls. You should thank whoever sent you here, because we're really not like any other."

He told her she would have a private room and assured her that if she had any problems with her accommodations, he could be reached during office hours on weekdays. They breezed down a corridor where several bedrooms were located. "The east wing of the house," he explained.

"It's big," she whispered in awe. Jaxon looked at the vaulted ceiling and wrapped her arms tighter around herself as she passed another open door. Frowning inhabitants peered back at her with distrust. The doctor strolled to the very end of the hall and opened the door to a small room that beckoned like an oasis in the desert.

"Take a look," he said. "This will be your new home for the next two years. As I said, it's a private room, but to be honest, you'll likely have a roommate soon. We generally stay at capacity. Now, I'll leave you to get settled in while I take care of some paperwork with your caseworker. You and I have a meeting at three o'clock. Please don't be late. Do you remember how to get to my office?"

"I think so."

"Excellent." He smiled, and his dark brown eyes were warm. Jaxon found herself smiling back. "I have a feeling this is going to be a life-changing experience for you. I can only hope you'll embrace the change. Have a good evening."

He put down her suitcase and ducked out of her room, leaving Jaxon standing at the threshold, peeking in. Her container was already in the room, and it looked un-tampered with. She took a tentative step onto the green carpet, feeling it sink underfoot, and her light blue eyes danced around the space, taking in the sights. Jaxon quietly shut her door behind her and leaned against the cool wood. The room was painted pristine white and had a newness to it.

Having come from homes where she'd had to share a bedroom with others or live in closet-sized quarters, she found the room a treat. Large enough for two beds, two desks, a large walk-in closet, and even a television stand, the bedroom seemed excessive compared to her standard fare.

Matching black duvets covered the twin beds positioned against the wall to her right, separated by a nightstand with an elegant rectangular lamp. Throw pillows on the beds were light green, like the carpet that covered the floor. Paintings hung on the walls—watercolors of flowers.

On the left, two small writing desks flanked the television stand. There were doors on either end of the wall—one to the closet and one to a personal bathroom. Jaxon bit her knuckle in anticipation as she tiptoed into the bathroom and looked around. It was painted a soft blue, tiled in matching blue and white, and a claw-foot tub dominated the design. A washbowl and toilet of her own. She wanted to jump with excitement. Jaxon was finding it hard to picture the place as punishment.

On closer inspection, the furniture and other elements of the room had a gently worn, secondhand feel, as if many others had shared the room before her. But the bedroom was clean and clearly well taken care of. The television was boxy and ancient, but when she hit the power button, it powered on in vivid high-definition. Jaxon let out a soft shriek of surprise and threw herself back on the bed closest to the window. She kicked off her shoes and squirmed around on the comfortable mattress.

Her racing heartbeat was beginning to slow, and her anxiety over the move—which she had hidden well, even from herself—gradually diminished. Jaxon stared at the television screen and let the cartoon watch her as she drifted off in thought. She understood the group home likely had its low points, too. She knew that she had yet to meet another member of the household, but she didn't care, because she also understood that as long as she had that room to return to, she might have finally found a sanctuary. And that was more than she had ever had at any other time and at any other place.

She smiled to herself, feeling... at home.

Chapter 2

MARCH 14, 2016, SAN FRANCISCO,
CALIFORNIA

2:55 PM

Dr. Hollis had an office on the first floor, and it was more like an oversized closet than a full-fledged room. Tucked into a corner of the house at the end of the entryway, the office was partitioned from the foyer by a wall with a rounded arch. Jax ambled down the stairs at the appointed hour of their meeting, wondering idly how anyone ever imagined they would get any privacy while chatting with the good doctor with such an open floor plan. Passers-by in the hallway could clearly see into the room and listen to whatever was being discussed. She nervously peeked past the arch.

The floor of the office was dark hardwood, and the walls were eggshell white with built-in bookshelves loaded with books and an assortment of odds and ends. There was barely enough room for the few pieces of furniture. Beyond the entrance was a high-backed settee in faded scarlet damask, stuffy and old-fashioned, with a secondhand patina. In front of the settee was a small round coffee table inlaid with glass and covered in a thick layer of dust. It sat low, and a bronze floor lamp was placed against a wall beside it.

She cautiously entered and waited to be noticed. Dr. Hollis sat at a battered old desk in front of an oak door. The door boasted a stained glass window filtering in soft, colorful light, and the door appeared to lead outside. It seemed an odd place to block off. His desk was littered with loose papers, and sticky notes were tacked to his computer monitor. He was scribbling furiously in a notebook. Jaxon cleared her throat, but he didn't seem to hear.

"Dr. Hollis?" She spoke softly so as not to disturb him.

The doctor glanced up from his notebook with a distracted expression. "Ah, Jaxon! Come in, come in. Give me a moment. I was just... just finishing up some progress notes, bothersome paperwork." He shifted in the busted leather office chair and went back to his notes as Jaxon nervously perched in a rounded dining room chair near his desk. She glanced around the room to get a feel for the man who would be her new therapist.

In her sixteen years, she had had her share of psychiatrists, psychologists, and psych nurses. She had so much experience with them, she almost felt she could read them as well as they pretended to read her. For instance, a lot could be discerned about a person from a thorough examination of their environment.

Dr. Hollis's office indicated no conscious effort at decorating. The furniture was a motley mix of pieces, many of which didn't belong in an office. He clearly had no design theme, unless it was "bored bachelor slaps together a room." Jax bit her lips to keep from smiling. An olive green carry-on bag was bunched beneath the settee. A lone black file cabinet was beside the desk, and an accent chair was tucked in a corner, both piled with books and notebooks. What looked like a clothes hamper filled with magazines was in the other corner by the entry arch behind her. There was no order.

The wastebasket overflowed, and dust covered more than just the coffee table. Dr. Hollis seemed to have grown into his space, however, as if he had been at the facility long enough to dig roots in deep. There were many personal touches such as houseplants and photographs on the shelves. Behind him was a tacky poster of a snowflake with the words "Thank You" above Japanese script.

Jax determined he was a single-focus man, prone to forgetfulness and absent-ed-mindedness, judging by the sticky-note reminders and apparent disregard for cleanliness. He probably couldn't walk and chew bubblegum at the same time. He was a studied man, she decided as she judged his taste in reading. Most of the books were academic in nature, spines lined and creased from frequent handling. He spent either way too much time in his office or not enough.

"Thank you," he murmured without looking up, "for your patience. These damn deadlines always catch up with me before I'm ready."

"It's no problem." A half smile curled her lips upward.

He dotted the last *i* and crossed the last *t*. "Now that that's over with, the first order of business is to get you an ID card. After that, we'll get you tested and placed. Um, is this your first group home?" Dr. Hollis was flipping papers and folders on his desk, hunting for Jaxon's. He impatiently ran his thin fingers through his wavy, longish brown hair, eyebrows knit together over his aquiline nose. He finally found the file tucked in the top drawer where he had placed it to keep from losing it.

"Yep." Jax pursed her lips and slouched in her chair, tapping the armrests with her fingertips.

Dr. Hollis turned his computer toward her. "Smile for the camera." A wavering twist of her lips was captured by the quick flash, and Jaxon inwardly groaned at what was bound to be a terrible identification badge photo. Dr. Hollis toyed with his mouse and keyboard for a few minutes before the card maker attached by USB port spit out a flat, rectangular card.

"That's it?" Jaxon asked as he handed the card across the desk.

"That's all there is to that. Make sure you keep up with the card because I have to charge you five bucks for every replacement. You'll need it to access the dining hall and classroom. You'll be pleased to find out we also have a recently renovated game room and snack shop on the top level. Your ID card can be loaded with FW points to be used up there."

"How do you earn FW points?"

"Every student starts off with ten FW points. You can earn them and lose them according to your behavior. You earn more by doing noteworthy things around the house. Your teachers and other staff members all score your positive behavior weekly and enter their appraisals via computer, resulting in points added to your account. Kind of like a bank deposit." He held up a warning finger. "Similarly, infractions result in loss of points. I'll give you our handbook before you leave so you can familiarize yourself with our expectations."

"So if I break the rules, I just get points taken away?" She snickered, clamping down on her lips before laughing outright.

Dr. Hollis gave her a harsh look. "We don't like to operate under a system of punishments here. We prefer rewarding good behavior rather than promoting irresponsible behavior by making a spectacle of a misstep. However, rest assured, any resident caught breaking the rules will be dealt with summarily. Now"—he brightened—"ready to get the testing over with?"

"Is it some sort of formal process with papers and bubble sheets? Or do you just bombard me with meaningless questions and pictures and fudge my responses? How does it work?" Jaxon thought testing was a waste of time. She sighed gustily and crossed her arms.

Dr. Hollis chuckled, shaking his head. He reached behind him for a cracked and torn binder atop the black file cabinet. "Basically, closer to the latter. Let me explain. Our residents receive homes-chooling, and our curriculum doesn't mirror what you'd see in a typical public school. Rather, we format lesson plans according to an IEP. Do you know what that is?"

"I think I had one before." Jax rolled her eyes. "I'm dyslexic. Individual education program."

"Right! Precisely. The lesson plans are structured to strengthen your weaknesses and cater to your strengths. Listen, we're not here to make it harder to learn. We're here to make it easier for you to process and utilize new information. So let's start with some aptitude tests and see where we can go from there. Let me warn you, this is going to take a while."

"Like, how long?"

He shrugged, looking apologetic. "Depending on some of your results, it could take much of the rest of the evening and possibly a portion of tomorrow morning. But don't worry. I'll have you settled into your courses soon and get you started with our program in no time. You trust me on that?" He smiled warmly, and Jaxon felt her lips twitch in response. He had an infectious smile.

"I guess I don't have a choice."

He placed a small voice recorder on the center of his desk and angled it toward her. Then he turned his computer camera to face her so he could record video. Jaxon fidgeted in the uncomfortable dining chair. She hated being the center of attention.

Dr. Hollis started the psychometric testing with general achievement and intelligence tests, diligently making notes. Jaxon watched his face run the gamut of emotions from intrigue to intense surprise at some of her responses.

Jaxon knew she would score high on the charts intellectually, and in a rare move, she answered to the best of her ability—and the best of her ability was far from average. Jax didn't know why she was giving Dr. Hollis preferential treatment. Ordinarily, getting answers from her was next to impossible. By the end of the aptitude tests, he looked stunned.

"Wow. You're really quite amazing," he said.

Jaxon blushed, gnawing on her bottom lip. "Is that a bad thing here?"

His eyebrows shot up over his glittering brown eyes. "Why on earth would it be?" He shook his head, realization dawning. "Ah, of course. You must be wondering if you'll catch any flak from the other students for your intelligence metrics. No, no, we have a no-bullying policy here, and please don't limit yourself on account of others. Do you know your IQ? Gosh, I almost want someone else to readminister the test just to be sure I haven't made any errors."

"It's not that big of a deal," said Jaxon, shrugging. She wrapped her arms around herself, wondering if she had made a mistake in revealing her true potential. "Nobody has to know, really."

"Jaxon, your IQ is about 172. To put that into perspective, Einstein's was 160."

"Are you serious?" she whispered.

He waved his hands in front of him. "I mean, you can fail every other test you take in class, but intelligence like that is hard to hide. I'm kind of blown away right now." He hooted and muttered, "Sheesh, you're smart enough to take my job."

She giggled. He cleared his throat and made a long face, flashing her a playful grin. "Who am I kidding? Who the heck wants my job? But realistically speaking, I've looked at your transcripts, and you were definitely underperforming. Have you put any thought into college or anything like that? What do you want to do when you get out of here?"

Jaxon shrugged. She hadn't thought about what she would do when she left the foster care system. She had a vague vision of herself working in Walmart or some other store, making enough money for a studio apartment somewhere where she could do whatever the hell she wanted with her life, which was... well, anything other than being told what to do. She shrugged again.

Dr. Hollis steepled his fingers atop his desk and gazed at her warmly. "I want you to start formulating a five-year plan. Sounds extreme, I know, but five years can pass in the blink of an eye, and if you don't know where you plan to go, you don't know where you'll end up. I want you to make a list of colleges or trade schools you want to apply to, and I want you to construct a game plan for how you intend to improve your grades so you can meet the standards required."

"Man, you're asking a lot of me."

"I expect a lot, now that I know what you can do. All right, back to the business at hand. I'm going to read a few questionnaires to you. Ready?" Dr. Hollis rose from his chair and pointed a thumb toward the door. "Want to go out back? It gets stuffy in here around this time of day."

"Sure," Jaxon murmured. The psychiatrist powered off the voice recorder and stuck it into his pocket. He turned off the camera and beckoned her to follow him.

"Tell me why you had such a hard time at your last school," he said as he wrestled open the door.

Jaxon sighed and replied, "Virtually every school I've attended has been the same. Everywhere I go, I have people on my case. They talk about me, try to fight me. 'Cause people tend to underestimate me. I'm small, you know."

Dr. Hollis chuckled, nodding understandingly. He got the door open only wide enough for them to squeeze through, their access hampered by the placement of his desk. She shimmied through the crack behind him.

"'And, though she be but little, she is fierce.' William Shakespeare wrote that," he said. Jaxon's gaze flew to his face where his eyes crinkled gently in a relaxed smile as they headed out to the yard.

Jaxon was stunned. The backyard was expansive, its manicured lawn gleaming emerald green and bordered by gemstone flowers and lush shrubbery. An oversized ginkgo tree grew to the left of the open expanse, and picnic tables sat beneath the tree. Beyond the ginkgo was a volleyball net and plenty of room for outdoor play, but that wasn't what caught her eye.

The Forever Welcome gardens were unlike any she had ever seen. Ruby-red tulips vied with pearlescent oleander and topaz mums. Leafy jade sedum and stalks of sapphire indigo circled the yard. A high stone fence covered in climbing green ivy separated the backyard from the rest of the estate, and through a trellised archway covered with feathery wisteria was a cobblestone walkway that led to another enclosed garden. In the distance through the arch, she saw a massive fountain spewing glistening white water and more flowers and greenery. It beckoned.

Jaxon inhaled sharply as she admired the eye-popping vista. "What is this place?" she whispered breathlessly. She walked down the brick steps and along the stepping-stones toward the picnic tables, Dr. Hollis in her wake.

"Oh, this is the secret garden. Beautiful, isn't it?"

The sun was low in the dusky purple sky. It had to be near seven in the evening, but Jaxon wanted to keep going, the testing forgotten. She wanted to explore the verdant mystery beyond the brick wall. The muggy breeze was perfumed with floral scents and the smell of fresh-cut grass. The very act of breathing made her feel transported to another world where her earthly concerns were trivial. Jaxon closed her eyes and stood still next to the picnic table, immersing herself in the experience.

She could feel the garden's growth. She could literally feel the tingle through her shoes and against the pads of her toes and the balls of her feet. The hair along the back of her neck stood up, her heartbeat racing with an infusion of adrenaline. She was almost overwhelmed by the electric act of processing the assault to her senses. It was more than the beauty she could see, the aromas she smelled, and the warm breeze against her skin. There was something thought-provoking at play, something that teased at her mind with haunting fingers.

She couldn't place the sensation, but it was there.

Dr. Hollis gestured to the picnic table, drawing her attention away from the amazing view. He had his tablet computer and placed it on top of the table so they could continue the tedious testing, which wasn't so tedious since they were out of the office. Jaxon felt much more at ease. She studied the psychiatrist, a man unlike any other shrink she had ever encountered. She knew it was his job to peer into her brain and figure out all the things that were wrong with her, but he didn't seem to be doing that.

He reminded her of a character in a film, like Gregory Peck in *To Kill a Mockingbird*, with his charming good looks and gregarious personality. She stopped scrutinizing him when, during the next round of testing, his tone became more conversational. Dr. Hollis slid in a joke or two between the questions, and she found herself letting down her guard. Gradually, he broke from the question-naires and structured tests and made notes from her answers to his more personal questions.

"You're stronger than you appear, Jaxon Andersen."

"Stronger than you know," she said with a raise of her eyebrows and a half smile. She stared at the yard, and she wanted desperately to explore the grounds. She glanced back at Dr. Hollis and found him shaking his head and tapping his watch.

"Whoops! Look at me—I let time get away from me again. You're scheduled for dinner in less than thirty minutes."

"Dinner? Is it formal?" she asked anxiously. "Do I need to change?"

"No, not at all. Completely casual around here." He turned to go indoors. "Right this way, Jaxon. We'll have to complete the testing in the morning. Oh, and I have some forms, a welcome packet to give you. Let's see. Where did I put that stuff?" he muttered. Jaxon sighed and followed, reluctant to leave the garden that called to her in a language she almost recognized but couldn't quite comprehend. She peeked one last time over her slender shoulder then slipped inside.

Dr. Hollis was rifling through the papers on his desk. "I know I had that folder in here somewhere. Yellow, yellow, yellow..." Jaxon spotted a lemon-yellow folder on top of the accent chair and idly handed it to him. "Yes, there it is." He beamed excitedly, tapping the folder with widespread fingers. "In here is everything you need to know to get today finished and start your day tomorrow. Uh, there's information about the curfew, lights out, that sort of thing. And I think there's a map. Let me check. Ah yes, a map. Now, I had hoped to pair you with a mentor for your first few days here, but we're a little tight for staff, so you'll just have to rely on me."

He smiled self-deprecatingly, tilting his head and brushing back his long hair. He handed her the folder, and Jaxon stared down at it with a twinge of disappointment, daunted by the prospect of having to go through it. The yellow folder was thick as a book and jammed with papers and pamphlets. She hated reading. "Gee, thanks," she mumbled.

"Come along now. We'll be late to the dining hall if I don't get you there shortly."

He hurried off through the archway of his office and into the corridor that led to the staircase and entry foyer. Jaxon followed the psychiatrist through the front corridors of the great house. "There are currently nineteen residents, with you included. This is a coed facility, with males dorming on the west side of the house and females on the east, but residents eat together."

"Who supervises the dining hall? You said you were short-staffed." She was anxious about meeting the other residents. She wasn't in the mood to answer invasive questions or socialize or fend off taunts. The thought of dining with her peers took away her appetite entirely.

Dr. Hollis had a long-legged stride her shorter legs had trouble matching. She lagged behind as he zoomed ahead. "No, it doesn't quite work that way here. There is an appointed resident assistant for the boys and one for the girls, and the

RA maintains order during dining. The common areas of the facility are under video surveillance at all times. But you'll find this isn't an unruly lot. They're just like you, kids trying to mind their own business and get out of here." He coasted around a corner and waited for her.

"Let's remember I was sent here by the courts," Jaxon quipped dryly.

He chuckled. "They're not bad, Jaxon. I promise you, you'll get along fine. As for live-in staff, that would include the groundskeeper and the two housekeepers, who have cabins on grounds, as well as myself. The director is in the office every weekday from eight to four. We also have a rotating security staff. Previously, I had two interns working under me, but budget restraints being what they are..."

Dr. Hollis gestured to the set of white double doors, grasped the brass door handles, and shoved them inward. "Right through here." Sighing, Jaxon braced herself.

The dining hall wasn't exactly what Jaxon had imagined, based on the decor of the rest of the house. She had pictured a long dining table crowded with chairs. Instead, she saw five round mahogany tables with four upholstered chairs at each. The dining hall was on the east side of the house and overlooked a rustic covered patio. Beyond a wall of windows was another seating area outside on the patio, presumably for eating outdoors on a sunny day like today.

A few other residents were already seated around a table near the middle of the room. They looked up when Jaxon entered, and she wanted to shrink into herself to avoid their interest, but the two teenage girls and boy quickly returned to what they were doing, eating and conversing quietly.

Jaxon shuffled her feet at the threshold, not particularly ready to enter. Dr. Hollis looked back and caught her wandering eye, beckoning her forward. "You'll have to sign in first. Swipe your card here under the touchscreen." He pulled her over to a computer and tapped it out of sleep mode.

Jaxon dug the card from her pocket and ran it under the flickering blue light beneath the flat screen just beyond the double doors. "Excellent," said Dr. Hollis. "Over there along the main wall is the longboard table. For each meal, the chef prepares and lays out the buffet. You pick what you like, but we discourage waste around here. Please select only what you know you'll eat. Seconds are permitted, depending on availability, but you don't look like you eat more than a bird," he teased.

Jaxon blushed and followed him over to the assortment of covered dishes on the longboard. On the wall above the repast was a chalkboard listing the menu options. The day's dinner fare included pasta with meat sauce, meatballs and spring greens or vegan pasta, and sautéed mushrooms and spring greens. Several dessert choices were listed along with drinks ranging from green tea to soda. Beside the longboard was a crate of dinner plates and silverware.

"Think you can handle things from here?"

She smiled bravely and nodded. Jaxon refused to be defeated by a bout of nerves. With a resolute sigh, she grabbed a plate and selected a few items, ambling to an empty table and sitting down to eat. She had her folder to peruse. That would discourage anyone from talking to her.

"One day down," Jax muttered to herself. Two years to go.

Chapter 3

MARCH 14, 2016, SAN FRANCISCO, CALIFORNIA

8:00 PM

Anthony Hollis lived at Forever Welcome in an apartment annexed to the back third story of the main house. As evening deepened to night on the day new student Jaxon Ares Andersen had arrived at the group home, he shut off the lamp in his office and bundled up the stack of folders he had been working on. Anthony hurried up the two flights of stairs to his room. The doctor had a lot on his mind, or rather one thing in particular on his mind—a particular person—and that was Jaxon.

He had been blown away by her intelligence quotient, but there was more to the girl than secret genius. He had seen her files, and he knew her history. The pint-sized fighter was a force to be reckoned with. At her last school, in a fit of anger, she had broken the surface off a student's desk with nearly impossible strength as a result of an adrenaline rush. Anthony hoped he didn't have to deal with anything like that at his facility.

Anthony had his share of gifted students come through the doors of Forever Welcome. He had long felt there was a connection among high intellect, lack of intellectual stimulation, and delinquency. Still, he had never encountered quite such a brilliant mind.

Anthony closed the door to his studio apartment and strolled across the living room area to his wrought-iron bed. He dug around in his pocket for his cell phone, which was nowhere to be found. He rifled through the pile of papers on his nightstand. The phone fell to the floor and skittered under his bed, and he got on his hands and knees to dig it out so he could make a call.

Anthony needed a second opinion. In fact, he needed a listening ear in general. "Did you get her results, Brady?" He shifted the phone to the other ear and sat on the edge of his bed, kicking off his scuffed leather shoes and putting his feet up to settle in and chat. Brady Welsh was a trusted friend and fellow psychiatrist. If anyone would know what to do with the girl, he would.

"I watched the video you sent over, yes," Brady said. "I'd have to agree. She's definitely sharp. Have you considered putting her in advanced placement and college courses? She might benefit from the challenge. I can't imagine a girl with her mind suffering through a high school curriculum."

"I thought about that. Plus, frankly, I doubt if my teachers are up to her speed." Anthony chuckled and loosened his tie. He had also taken her through some psychological tests, the results of which bothered him more than he cared to admit. "She also shows signs of having paranoid delusions, worrisome inner dialogue. I thought maybe I should start her on something to stabilize her mood a little and—"

"Oh, Tony, every teenager I know is a little bit insane. Don't get bogged down with the technicalities, and stay away from drugs. We tell the buggers just say no, and then we shove the pills down their throats. No, no, that's not the best course of action. From what you emailed me about her history of multiple foster homes, it's a wonder she's as well adapted as you've indicated. Now, about the aptitude tests, I'd be happy to re-administer when you're ready."

"Of course that depends on funding, I'm afraid."

"Always funding. Well... and your personal hobbies with Emoto's less than scientific pursuits? How have your experiments been coming along with studying molecular changes to water molecules?" Brady teased.

Anthony smiled sheepishly. He had a personal preoccupation with the studies of Masaru Emoto, the late, great Japanese researcher and author who had studied the effects of human consciousness on the structure of water molecules. According to Emoto, bombarding water with positive thoughts and words could literally change the quality of the water. Polluted water would be made clean, and the evidence was in the snowflakes. Water molecules exposed to positive pictures, music, and words would result in more symmetric, visually appealing crystals than those exposed to negative thoughts.

"It might be pseudoscience to you, but I think I'm onto something. I have pans on the window ledge as we speak. Now, it's nothing that would hold up to peer review, I guess, but you have to admit it's an interesting hobby. I've been reciting a simple poem of praise to the water every morning. This is my third batch."

"Eh? Uh-huh, and what happened to the first two batches?"

"W-w-well—" Anthony sputtered as peals of laughter spilled from the phone. "Ha! Don't laugh, old buddy. Like I said, it's an interesting hobby. I've been using the water to nurture a few plants in the greenhouse, and I can tell you the control plants aren't doing nearly as well by comparison. Care to see pictures? I could send them to you."

Anthony smiled to himself as the conversation drifted to more personal concerns. He had a very demanding job. Forever Welcome often required his presence twenty-four, seven. He didn't mind, because the reclusive psychiatrist had an interesting network of coworkers and friends he kept in contact with via telephone and the Internet, but he rarely met with others in person.

Anthony Hollis, psychiatrist extraordinaire, had nearly crippling social anxiety. He preferred socializing with his pans of water, his plants, and his residents at the comfortable, cozy group home to socializing with others. However, it helped to have friends he could call on when he wanted an outside expert opinion. "All of this is in strictest confidence," he reminded Brady. Neither one considered that there wasn't much privacy in a phone call that could be tapped, recorded, and traced, or in an email that could be hacked. Their deepest truths were exposed, and they were none the wiser.

As they bid their farewells and made plans to chat again after the rest of Jaxon's testing was complete, Anthony got off the phone feeling he had accomplished something. He pulled out his laptop computer and got to work preparing her class schedule. FW had several private tutors who provided assistance with online classes, but he didn't think any of them would do. "No, Jaxon, I'm afraid you're on your own in this."

He chewed on the base of his stylus and continued plotting what her days would look like for the rest of the school year at Forever Welcome. She had come in on the tail end of spring semester, but he was confident she wasn't behind. Anthony followed Brady's advice and signed her up for online AP courses. When he finished creating the necessary log-ins and activation codes, he put aside his computer and prepared for bed.

It was demanding work and lonely work, but it was rewarding. He couldn't wait to see how the wildflower Jaxon Andersen would fare under his tutelage and care. Anthony Hollis was more excited than he had been at any other point in his career, and it had everything to do with his new charge. She was special. And it was up to him to get the world to recognize that.

Chapter 4

MARCH 15, 2016, ALBUQUERQUE,
NEW MEXICO

7:45 AM

On a Tuesday morning one month into the project, Akiko Yamazaki was still getting used to the harrowing process of getting on campus at Starke Genetics & Development in Albuquerque, New Mexico.

Akiko wasn't a very young woman anymore, but she wasn't a very old woman, either. She was thirty-nine, and she had a life outside of her time-consuming research and professorial work at the university. Somewhat reclusive, she had an apartment near the university campus and was allowed to return home after her meeting with General Meade to pack her things for the temporary move to New Mexico. Asked if she would be willing to move into the compound to take part in the special operations General Meade wanted to recruit her for, Akiko had declined.

She was afraid of disappearing in the compound. She much preferred to clock in and out every day like everyone else. It was bad enough she had to relocate.

At an outer gate, her vehicle was required to display a windshield sticker, and she had to flash her ID badge. At the inner gate, security checked her vehicle, an assessment much like getting frisked by TSA at the airport. Finally, a number of access codes and card swipes later, she was allowed to walk into the building.

Officially, the name of the place was Starke Genetics & Development. It was an ordinary steel and glass building used for ordinary scientific research. Unofficially, Akiko was working on top-secret government research. She wasn't allowed to talk about it, write about it, or even think about it off grounds, and it all had to do with her prior projects delving into ancestral DNA analysis.

"Tell me how it works again?" General Meade had been inquisitive the first day they met.

Akiko had explained, "In the simplest terms possible, much like scientists can tell a lot about you from your DNA, scientists can also tell a lot about your parents from your DNA. Now divide that by generations and generations, and one can quite accurately pinpoint your ancestral origins. What I do is forward track. I start with the ancestors and decode their DNA to understand more about older civilizations."

"Doesn't seem like there would be much use for that kind of thing in this day and age." He chuckled. General Meade was a technology man, himself. He liked his futuristic tech and gadgets. What the doctor was talking about was ancient history. "More specifically, tell me about your current project."

Akiko blushed, reluctant to lay it all on the line. Her colleagues had already scoffed at her. Very few at the research university where she held tenure understood her work, and those that did felt she might be barking up the wrong tree, but she heaved a sigh and attempted to explain to the general what she wanted to do and why it was important.

"There is much use for it in this day and age. For starters, analyzing the genetic differences between ancient civilizations and comparing them to changes across the population today yields valuable information about some of our rarest genetic disease, mutations, and marvels. For example, some are genetically predisposed to Alzheimer's while others are not. Have you ever wondered why? I have, and I know—theoretically—why. It all traces back to our ancient origins."

"Your current project, though?" General Meade prompted. He hated doctors. They got so consumed with spouting on about their special interests that it was impossible to keep them on track. But he needed this particular doctor. No one else could do what she was doing. He was well aware of that because he had scoured the country for someone with her expertise, and she stood out like a diamond in the rough.

"My current project deals not just with ancient but also with extinct civilizations. Now, you might ask how we can even obtain modern DNA samples from civilizations that are extinct. After all, there wouldn't be any descendants, right However, what we can do is study those from the same general geographical area. In 2001, I worked on a project studying the genetic material of the Nahua people of Middle America in attempts at finding evidence of links to the Aztecs. Essentially, it's incredibly difficult to wipe out every single person of a population. The Aztec culture was wiped out, but some Nahua ancestors were likely a branch who survived the Spaniard invasion."

"I see, I think."

"So you see, studying modern populations, accounting for migrational patterns over centuries, allows us a starting point to trace back to ancient, even extinct civilizations. But why the sudden interest, General Meade? I'm not in the habit of playing nice with government agents in black cars—men in black. I'm not sure I can trust you."

"What you can trust," he said casually, "is that no resource will be spared in getting you every single thing you need to successfully research and document the genetic material of the population you're seeking. You realize that without our help, it might have taken you a lifetime to find a handful of participants to study, right? But with my help, you'll be riding the crest of success in no time."

"I haven't told you which population I'm seeking, General..."

"I know these things, Dr. Yamazaki. It's my job to know."

The black sedan had left the university campus and traveled to an airport in Arizona before flying her to a secret government-run facility in Utah. There, she sat in on a meeting with General Meade and several other officials, including the intelligence analyst who had compiled "the list." The meeting lasted several hours, little of it concerning her, but at length it was Dr. Yamazaki's turn to speak. When she stepped to the podium, she felt the urgency of the situation. If she could convincingly outline her project to these important men, it could mean the difference between success and failure.

Akiko wasn't idealistic. She understood her research required money, and she understood that, sometimes, getting the money to do her research required holding hands with less than desirable friends, like General Meade. That said, she would be his friend and use his resources to conduct her research. In the back of her mind, she wondered again why the military would be interested in her results.

"Ancient civilizations... today. The two concepts seem at odds, but they're not," said Akiko. "Popular culture still maintains an avid interest in ancient civilizations as evidenced by all the movies, books, and music about such extinct peoples. I am an anthropologic geneticist, not a movie director, however. My own interest is with a very specific ancient civilization, one some say never existed at all. In 360 BC, Plato first referenced a debatable lost city, the domain of Poseidon, an island nation in the Atlantic Ocean populated by a powerful race of advanced people."

The gentlemen murmured as they began to discuss the implications of what they thought she was about to say. The terms *Plato* and *lost city* were dead giveaways. Akiko braced herself for the backlash.

"Continue," said General Meade, shushing his companions.

Akiko took a deep breath and blurted out, "The Lost City of Atlantis. Plato's tale has long been believed to refer to the destroyed Minoan civilization, an equally advanced and sophisticated culture. Atlantis might even be fiction and have never existed. Or the real Atlantis might still be visible today as the Azores islands, believed to be the tip of the submerged city. Frankly, I'm not here to theorize the original location of the City of Atlantis. I am here to discuss a particular genetic study which put Atlantis on the map for me."

She cleared her throat and took a sip of water, perusing the notes she'd been allowed to hastily compile from her office in Arizona before the flight. "I received a sample of material from an Egyptian mummy buried in a tomb inscribed with the Egyptian hieroglyph for Atlantis. As you may know, Plato ascribed the original story of Atlantis to the Egyptians. With this sample, I was able to pull a small amount of mitochondrial DNA, and I discovered something I'd never seen before. It wasn't quite... human."

There were chortles of amusement and shaking heads. Akiko's lips turned up in a half smile. She had come too far to turn back. She dropped her head and studied her notes again, her voice lowering as she pressed on. "I considered it a fluke until I came across a similar DNA signature in another patient years later. I was called in to consult on a case concerning a young man by the name of Lance Pierson. He suffered a rare genetic disease a colleague of mine felt might be the result of what he called the patient's 'unusual DNA.' He also suffered psychiatric symptoms and delusions. Pierson believed he could transmute electromagnetic energy."

She would never forget the case or the young man, though the patient had disappeared back into obscurity after her part in analyzing his DNA was completed. He had claimed to have unique abilities and was branded a lunatic, but Akiko hadn't been fully convinced he was crazy. She had seen it with her own eyes—he could *do* things. And that had prompted her lifelong interest in how many more people like him were out there in the world.

"My goal," Akiko said with renewed confidence, "is to prove the existence of the lost city by locating and studying descendants of the extinct Atlantean civilization. I believe there are more like Lance Pierson out there, more like the Egyptian mummy from the tomb with the Atlantis hieroglyphic. I believe the evidence of their existence manifests mentally and behaviorally. To test my theories, I will need a sizable sample population that I don't have, but you seem to. What I do have is the Mother copy, and you won't find that anywhere else in the world."

Now, here she was, working with the Poseidon Project at a research facility in New Mexico with the list of potential descendants. Akiko should have been happy, but she wasn't. She felt conflict- ed. She couldn't decide if what they were doing was entirely ethical. Yet in the name of science, it seemed the only way to get the answers she so desperately sought.

The goings-on in the secret facility weren't exactly popular in the surround- ing community. Rumors of genetic exper- iments and things that go bump in the night made the laypeople suspicious of those they considered scientists playing God. Akiko had no interest in doing what the rumormongers accused—creating strange, new variations of human beings, genetic splicing and the like. Her only purpose at the facility was to quickly, quietly, and thoroughly go through "the list."

"I guess the ends justify the means," she muttered to herself. She stood patiently waiting in the foyer beyond the building's heavy glass doors while the security team patted her down.

"What was that, Dr. Yamazaki?" asked the man in blue.

"Nothing, nothing. Are we done?" It was an intrusive process, but Akiko understood the need. Some things in the tall building shouldn't get out, and some things shouldn't get in. Finally, the security team waved her through the scanner and allowed Akiko through the imposing columned entrance of Starke Genetics.

The place was snazzy. The decor was ultramodern, and the ground level had walls paneled in Brazilian teak with granite flooring. The waiting area had a mix of chrome and black leather furniture tucked to one side of the lobby, and to the other side, an open corridor led deeper into the medical floor where examination rooms were located behind steel doors. On higher levels were doctors' offices and laboratories. Akiko walked from the main lobby through the glossy corridor and headed to the elevator bay at the end of the hall. The walkway overlooked the front of the building, windows letting in light. Overhead, the ceiling was a cross-hatch of wooden beams, and the floor beneath her heels was dull gray stone.

Akiko wore a white lab coat over her black pantsuit and held nothing in her hands. She wasn't allowed to bring anything on the grounds or to take anything away. She pushed her long black hair out of her face and peered ahead with her dark brown eyes. "Going down? Hold that, please!" she called out. She breezed into the elevator, smiling appreciatively at the lab tech traveling with her to the basement of the facility, where the department for the Poseidon Project was located.

It felt like being a member of a secret society. Akiko had been at the facility for a month and was still no closer to knowing her coworkers, other than her personal lab assistant, James Yuhle, whom she had convinced Meade to allow to come with her.

"Morning, Yuhle," she greeted him as she walked into the sterile glass room.

"We got more names on the list." The young doctor looked up from his microscope and pushed his glasses higher, smiling at the sight of her. A shadow of a beard covered his rounded cheeks and chin, his wavy sandy-brown hair falling over his forehead. He was gangly and looked barely old enough to have a license, much less a doctorate. Akiko graced him with a warm grin before sighing and taking a seat in front of her computer to go through the list of subjects they had already tested.

"Are we done with the last ones?" she asked. They had analyzed the results of over three hundred patients. It was time-consuming work that required an entire team dedicated to the testing—and a state-of-the-art laboratory—but they had done it. Yet as quickly as they eliminated names from the list, Meade and his trusted intelligence analyst found more people to add. It was daunting but rewarding work. Akiko hadn't found the needle in the haystack she was searching for, but she was confident she would, at the rate they were going.

"You ever wonder why they want to find these people?" Yuhle asked softly.

They were alone in her office, but Akiko shot him a look. "Not here," she murmured in warning. It wasn't wise to ask questions like that of the powers that be who were funding her research, but she did wonder. General Meade was military, working in conjunction with the National Security Agency to seek people with unique genetic material and purportedly unique special abilities. She thought again of Lance Pierson and how he had fallen off the map after his talents were discovered. It was unsettling.

"It doesn't matter why *they* want to find these people," she said with a shake of her head. "What matters is why *we* want to find them. This is a rare opportunity to study the difference between their genetic material and ours."

"Us versus them? So, you really think they're that much different from us?"

Akiko grinned excitedly, nodding. She pulled up another work screen and prepared to go through the graphics from the lab results. "I've seen it with my own eyes, Yuhle," she stated proudly. "They're not like us... they're much, much more advanced than we'll evolve to be for probably another million years."

"And it all traces back to the ancient Atlanteans."

"That's just a theory, a catchy headline. I have no idea of their origin. All I know is, I've only ever encountered the one patient. Here's hoping he wasn't the only one."

Chapter 5

MARCH 15, 2016, SAN FRANCISCO,
CALIFORNIA

7:45 AM

Jaxon had unpacked in the night, and her sparse wardrobe barely filled the new closet and dresser. It was her second day at the group home, and she dug out a white cotton shift and pulled it over her head. She surveyed her appearance in the mirror hanging from the back of her door, wanting to make a good impression on the students she'd be rubbing elbows with throughout the rest of the day.

There she was, same as always. The same indeterminable race, with a complexion that could be African-American, or Latina, or probably biracial, which still raised the question, what racial mix? She had slightly slanted eyes and thick, lustrous black hair that was too coarse to be fine but too fine to be coarse.

When she was younger, Jaxon had been preoccupied with tracing her elusive roots, but the trail always stopped at a dead end. She knew that as a nine-month-old, she was abandoned in a stranger's car in a shopping center parking lot, rescued from heatstroke by the owner of said car, and carted off to the Family Support Service. There was no paper trail to track down the name of her mother and no way to find out about her father. It was disheartening. She didn't belong to anyone.

Jax shook her head at her reflection, tired of wondering about herself and deciding she looked passable. It was time to get the day started. According to the weighty yellow folder jam-packed with the FW handbook and welcome materials, she had group therapy from seven to nine in the morning, but not that morning. Jaxon had a message from

Dr. Hollis to meet him in his office for the rest of her testing and to get her class assignments.

She didn't have a backpack, and she figured she probably didn't need one. Jax slipped her dainty feet into a pair of brown sandals and opened the bedroom door to see who else was up and about and moving around. There were voices in the hall. "Hi," she murmured shyly to a girl heading down the stairs ahead of her.

"Hey, yourself. You're the new kid?"

Jaxon shrugged. "I guess so."

The other girl nodded and continued down the hall to the great room. Jaxon followed because she still wasn't quite familiar with the layout of the house. She discovered the group was held there, and she watched several other residents ignore her and duck through the archway into the room. Jax ambled back down the corridor to the foot of the stairs, remembering Dr. Hollis's nook was through the archway at the opposite end of the hall.

"Good morning, Jaxon," he greeted from his desk.

Jaxon peeked over her shoulder at the students trudging to the great room and turned back to his office, where she was safe from contact with them. "Hey." She walked to the dining chair in front of his cluttered desk and took a seat. "So, let's get this over with."

"We were going to do a few more questionnaires geared toward building a personality profile on you, but I really don't think that will be necessary right now. That is, not unless we see you having problems adapting to the new environment. What do you think?" Dr. Hollis had made a decision overnight that he hoped he wouldn't regret. Dr. Brady was right. He was sometimes a stickler for technicalities, and there was enough data compiled that he didn't need to pick Jaxon's brain to find something wrong with her.

She shrugged, taken aback at being asked to evaluate for herself whether she needed further testing. "You're the doctor, aren't you?" she replied quizzically.

Dr. Hollis smiled encouragingly, gesturing for her to give him more feedback. "Yes, yes, but this is your life experience we're talking about here. I'm really just asking if you want to stall a little longer or if you're ready to get your courses and get out there and meet some people. I let you go too late in the evening yesterday for you to do much mingling."

"Oh, no, no. I'm not in a rush. I'm kind of a loner. I don't know if you read my history, but I, eh, don't play well with others." The corners of her lips turned upward in an amused smirk. She had already told him about some of the trouble she had had in her foster homes. No surprise there.

Dr. Hollis spent the next half-hour explaining the sign-in process so when classes started, she could access her terminal and get to her platform. He used his laptop computer to show her how to get to the website. "Online courses?" she said with interest. "I thought we all had private tutors or whatever."

"You do. Well, actually, you don't." He looked skyward and tried again. "Let me explain. All of the students are assigned a personal tutor to assist where needed as they go through their weekday classes. We've got residents ranging in age from twelve to eighteen, so their academic levels are diverse. You, on the other hand, won't really need that."

Dr. Hollis leaned back in the busted leather chair and surveyed the pretty honey-brown girl sitting across from him. She looked uncomfortable in her own skin, and he hoped he could eventually change that. He had helped hundreds of students matriculating in and out of the group home over the course of his ten years working there. He understood that some of the greatest challenges troubled children faced were their own self-criticisms. It was his goal to be a mirror reflecting positive potential rather than just another naysayer.

"You're far more advanced than any of the students here." He smiled, shaking his head, still amazed by that. He had seen her transcripts from her previous schools. She was a D-average student, barely above failing, yet she was literally a genius. "Your curriculum is a mix of advanced placement high school classes and college-level classes. You could probably take all college-level courses, but there are some of the others you have to take to get your high school diploma."

"But my dyslexia," she countered. "Sure, I can do well when you call the test questions out and I answer verbally, but it all goes to shit on paper."

"Whoops. Swear bucket. You just got a point docked."

"What?" She covered her mouth.

"Sorry about that. You'll see the point loss reflected on your weekly email summary of your FW points. We discourage informal language such as swearing around here. It might take a little time to get used to it, but you will get used to it. Swearing isn't allowed." Jaxon scowled. How the hell—heck—had she already lost a point? She'd probably end up broke by the end of the week. She sighed and crossed her arms.

"Where were we?" Dr. Hollis glanced down at his desk and patted the papers. "Ach, dyslexia! So, I've arranged for a colleague of mine, an educational psychologist, to work personally with you via daily hour-long sessions separate from the rest of your class time. The goal is to teach you different ways of learning to process written information. I've developed an individual education plan to address your needs. To be honest, I don't think you're going to have much of a problem."

Jaxon shook off her ire at losing FW points and perked up with interest at the prospect of having a specialized curric-ulum—complete with specialists—to help with her disability. "I've always felt a little slow for not being able to read like others, although I kinda knew I was smart, you know?" She stared down at her hands. When she looked up at Dr. Hollis, his dancing brown eyes matched the ever-present smile on his ruddy face, and he seemed to agree that she was smart. Jax wasn't used to teachers or therapists having confidence in her.

"Which just goes to show you that the concept of intelligence is complex. Certainly, understanding of language is a key component of intellectual ability, but the brain is a many-splendored thing. If I may say so, yours is a multifaceted jewel. Don't let your hang-ups about your learning disorder affect your self-esteem. You're a marvel, Jaxon."

She smiled shyly, flattered.

"So, you'll use your ID badge—do you have it with you? Ah, yes, you remem-bered it. Perfect—to access the computer lab. Teagan, one of your classmates, will be your guide today. I've arranged for her to break with group early to take you on a walk around the place." He patted around the desk, searching for the slip of paper where he had written her access codes. It was tucked beneath his coffee mug, and when he pulled it free, there was a brown ring. "Yikes, sorry about that," he muttered.

"Don't worry about it," she responded, accepting the paper by the tip of her fingers. Jaxon hated disorderliness, but Dr. Hollis was all right. She could put up with his less than neat ways. "I take it I'm supposed to go to group now?"

"Oh, and group therapy, let me explain that. Basically, every weekday morning, you and the rest of the residents in your age bracket, sixteen to eighteen, will meet up to discuss any problems you're having. They're really more like peer discussion sessions than group therapy. My schedule is"—he whistled—"hectic enough as it is without having to do that every morning, but! But I'm always available, should you need to talk. My door is always open. I don't even have a door. See?"

His speech was rapid, and he constantly shifted subjects. He gestured when he talked and invariably moved things around on his desk looking for something, but he had a harried quality about him, and she found him interesting to watch. He had a way of making her feel overwhelmed, as if she were late for an important meeting. Jaxon decided she liked Dr. Anthony Hollis. He was so very imperfect.

She rested her elbows on his desk and leaned forward, smiling. "Hopefully, this will be the easiest placement I've ever had, and you won't have to see me in here much." She was doubtful. Trouble seemed to find her everywhere she went. "Hopefully," she reiterated.

"That's the spirit. No trouble, no worries," he said with a grin. "But if you do have any problems, you know where to find me."

Jax avoided group by sneaking off to breakfast, and when she came out of the dining hall, she noticed the classroom door. Stepping into the room after passing her access badge under the entry card reader was like walking into an office building. Located at the back of the house just beyond the dining room on the east side, the classroom was a bland break with the homey environment of the rest of Forever Welcome. The white walls and hardwood floors invited no distractions. Even the windows were covered with opaque blinds.

The classroom consisted of workstations, twenty cubicles in total, with five workstations in each of the four rows. The rows were separated by a narrow aisle in the middle of the room. Students were assigned their seats by grade level, with younger students to the front of the class and older students to the back. Jaxon hurried to her seat, the second to last computer with the sixteen- to eighteen-year-olds. The rest of the cubicles were already filled with students who had arrived early.

She hadn't taken the opportunity to meet anyone. She was studiously avoiding the other residents. But as Jax plopped down into the swivel chair and powered up her monitor, she discovered she was the center of attention. She tried to ignore the whispers and the eyes glancing in her direction. Some of the younger students peered over the tops of their cubicles to get a good look.

"Here we go," Jaxon muttered under her breath with a roll of her eyes.

"What's your name, New Girl?"

The taunting voice came from a gangly, pimply-faced boy with a crew cut who was wearing baggy jeans. He had beady blue eyes and an upturned nose. Jaxon sighed. Slouching, he strolled over to her area and parked his arm on top of her cubicle wall, leering down at her. "I saw you when you got here yesterday. What you in for?"

"None of your business." She barely moved her lips, and she kept her eyes on her computer screen. Using the coffee-stained slip of paper containing her passwords and access codes, she entered the information into her computer and watched the screen load with a welcome message. Jaxon eyed the small print, the letters jumbled.

"Figured you'd come to group this morning and get to know us and shit."

"Swear bucket," Jaxon muttered.

He chuckled nastily, leaning over her. "That only works for the teachers, wiseass. So, what's your name again?" Slowly, he perused her from head to toe. Jaxon avoided eye contact. Where was the supervision in this place? Wasn't she sent to the group home so she could be watched? She sighed heavily and tried to ignore the menace. "What's the matter, baby? Cat got your tongue?" he jeered.

"She thinks she's better than us," a feminine voice said. Snickers followed. Jaxon cringed. The girls were always so much worse than the boys. Jaxon chanced a glance and noticed that the culprit was the girl sitting across from her in the first cubicle on the other side of the room. With a mouthful of braces and glistening auburn hair cut in layers to frame her pretty face, she was clearly one of the popular ones. Jax groaned inwardly.

Talkative Much continued, "Couldn't come to group and hang out with the commoners. Had to spend the morning in the doctor's office with a sour disposition. She's the shrink's pet."

"He-he! Shrink's pet. Hey, doesn't she kind of look like a Chihuahua? Like a teacup Chihuahua! Little b—"

"All right, class, let's get to our places!" The clip of heels entering the room got everyone's attention, and suddenly the sharks circling her cubicle for blood swam off to their respective spots. Jaxon breathed a sigh of relief. She wasn't one to be intimidated. She just didn't want to have to put anybody in their place so early in the game. Why was it so hard for people to leave her alone?

Jaxon learned several important things on her first day of school at Forever Welcome. First, as with all good things, there was a flip side. Forever Welcome had its charms and its challenges. Second, like every other place she had been, the group home would have jerks who had a problem with her for absolutely no reason at all. And third, sitting in front of a computer for nearly eight hours with only intermittent breaks would be torture to her ADHD.

She tapped her foot restlessly and fidgeted in the chair. She swiveled aimlessly, chewing at a loose fingernail and sneaking peeks at what everyone else was doing.

As Dr. Hollis had indicated, four tutors alternated throughout the day, walking the aisles of the classroom. The learning time was mostly a quiet, solitary interaction between student and computer, but Jaxon also heard whispered conversations and the buzzes and chirps of cell phones as text messages were sent. The teachers didn't seem to mind as long as the work—which she discovered they monitored remotely—was getting done.

Around the first fifteen-minute break at eleven, Jaxon felt a tap on her shoulder and looked up in alarm to see one of the teachers standing over her. Her name tag said Stacey, and she had wiry black dreadlocks piled atop her head in intricate loops and coils. "Are you having any trouble, Jaxon?"

"No, um, I'm just... getting used to..."

The teacher nodded understandingly and knelt down near her desk chair. "It can take a little getting used to, but we do expect you to complete the assignments. Looks like, according to my synopsis, you're supposed to be answering the discussion questions from your AP English Lit class. You've been on the same screen for nearly an hour."

"I've got it covered," Jaxon growled, looking away. She had trouble with the reading. It was almost impossible to stay focused on the small font, and it was ludicrous of Dr. Hollis to expect her to segue right into college-level courses. *This is hopeless,* she thought, gnawing at her bottom lip angrily.

Stacey reached over Jaxon's keyboard and hit the control key, scrolling up with her mouse to make the font larger. Her walnut shell–brown face was freckled with hyper-pigmented moles. Stacey's full brown lips smiled gently, and her voice was mellow like the taste of saffron. She whispered to Jaxon, "As I understand it, you have dyslexia, right?" Jax nodded once, barely. She hated admitting her weaknesses. "Right," Stacey murmured. "Put on your headphones. They're located behind your monitor. You'll use the Ease of Access control panel to have highlight-ed text read to you." She patiently and discreetly showed Jaxon how to set the controls.

Jax felt tears of embarrassment well up in her eyes, but she mumbled, "Thanks."

"No problem. That's what I'm here for. If you have any other problems, you can press the help button in the upper right-hand corner of your desk. Once the button is depressed, the light atop your cubicle will illuminate to let me or one of the other teachers—Ms. Karen, Ms. Bhati, or Ms. Megan—know to come lend you a hand." She patted Jaxon's back and left her to her work.

Fifteen minutes later was the first break, and Jaxon escaped. "Where's the restroom?" she asked the quiet young man sitting to her left.

He mumbled directions, and Jax shot out of the classroom before anyone else could hold her up. She sat in an empty stall killing time and thinking about her morning. After the assistance from Ms. Stacey, she had labored through the reading assignment and answered one of the discussion questions.

She still had American History and her foreign language courses to complete, and then it would be time for lunch. She wondered what the catty crew would have in store once she was out of earshot of the teachers. Jaxon sighed and buried her face in her hands. She drew her slender fingers through her thick black hair and shook her head as she smashed her cheeks between her palms.

At that moment, the door to her stall came crashing in. "Hey!" Jax yelped.

"Look what I found. A dog doing her business on the toilet, like a human," the girl with the braces crowed. She was accompanied by two other girls, neither of whom appeared capable of thinking a single original thought, both of them tittering senselessly at the girl's crude joke.

Jaxon rose to her feet, fists balled. "Leave me alone," she growled.

"You made her bark, Lizzie!" One of the accomplices clapped her hands enthusiastically. "What else can you make her do?"

Jaxon shoved Lizzie out of her face and pushed out of the bathroom stall. She knew from experience never to let anyone back her into a corner. "You knuckle-draggers done talking? 'Cause I don't do speeches." Jax squared her shoulders, popped her neck, and put up her fists, bouncing on the balls of her feet. "I'm more hands-on."

Lizzie stepped back, howling with laughter. "I'm not fighting you, dogface." She flipped Jaxon off and shoved her shoulder as she strutted past. "Just stay out of my way, m'kay, girl? You're not worth my time. As in, I got just a few more months in this place, and I'm out."

Jaxon bristled, gunning for a fight but realizing Lizzie was the sort to bait rather than brawl, and the person who passed the first lick always got in more trouble than the person who started the fight. Jax grumbled under her breath and marched out of the bathroom with barely checked fury. No way would she run to Dr. Hollis's office like the shrink's pet they had accused her of being. But she wasn't about to put up with anyone's bull either. It was wonderful the girl with braces would be out soon because Jax didn't know how much longer she could bridle her fiery temper.

She breezed into the classroom and sat at her desk. She dug out her phone, but she didn't have anyone to call or text. Her smartphone was mostly for playing games and listening to music. Jaxon didn't have friends. She shook her head, angry all over again at what had happened in the bathroom. She didn't have friends because people were too busy trying to push her over the edge. It didn't matter anyway. Jax sighed. She was a loner by choice. It was easier. She was a rolling stone, a tumbleweed, never in one place for long, and that meant all of her problems were just passing through, too.

She got back to work on her assignments, and by the end of classes, she had survived the first day of school with barely a scrape. She could do it. She was built for it.

Chapter 6

APRIL 8, 2016, ALBUQUERQUE,
NEW MEXICO
1:00 PM

The male subject had been lured to the facility with a ruse. He was told he had won an all-expenses-paid safari vacation, but in order to prepare for the trip, he was required to go through a rigorous physical. His wife and three children had already been to the back room where their mouths were swabbed, blood was taken, and vitals were recorded. They were sent back out into the tastefully decorated waiting area, and then it was his turn.

"This will just take a second," said the nurse.

He opened his mouth, and she dug around his inner lip and cheek with a long cotton swab. The smell of her latex gloves assailed his nostrils. He hated that smell and wasn't too keen on hospitals in general. "I hope the trip is worth all this. Hey, aren't you supposed to give me vaccines and stuff? I heard somewhere they do that before trips to Africa."

The nurse pulled down her face mask and smiled. "Mr. Wilson, this is the preliminary exam. If we see any problems, we'll notify you and have you come back for a follow-up. As for vaccinations, I don't know anything about that, but I'm sure the doctor can answer any questions you have."

"And when do I see the doctor?" He winced as the nurse tightened the rubber tourniquet about his upper arm. She pressed his antecubital fossa, looking for a suitable vein, and he winced again as she inserted the needle.

Zion Wilson was glad when he hopped in his Yukon and drove back to his ranch house with the family. He had been informed all their results would be back within twenty-four hours. The sooner the results were in, the sooner they could start planning the vacation of a lifetime.

"...And elephants, and giraffes, and lions," his five-year-old daughter was running down the list of animals she hoped to see.

"Kizzy! Why do you talk so much?" his nine-year-old whined.

"All right, all right, simmer down. When we get inside, I want you to give your baby sister a bath, Denise. Your mom and I are gonna get dinner started."

"Fish tacos?" his wife suggested. He grinned at her and nodded.

"Sounds good to me."

They piled out of the SUV and filed into the house, where the kids argued about who would take a bath first, and he and his wife sauntered into the kitchen, ignoring the bickering.

Lorraine Wilson put her elbows on the kitchen counter and leaned over to talk to Zion. Her curly black hair was a halo around her olive face. "So, what do you think they were testing us for?"

Zion shrugged. "Beats me. Said they'll call if they see any problems." He cupped her face and kissed the tip of her nose. "But there aren't gonna be any problems. In a few months, we'll be in the middle of Africa, riding across the savanna, taking pictures of the elephants, giraffes, and lions." He chuckled softly.

By the next day, he was no longer laughing. He was back at Starke Genetics & Development, wearing a worried frown. Tension in his shoulders and neck made his head ache, and when the nurse called him back to the examination room, his legs were shaking. He had received the callback while at work, and the friendly nurse on the other end of the line had assured him he didn't have anything grave to worry about, so he hadn't told his wife.

He couldn't imagine explaining to Lorraine that some health concern might hold up their trip. Zion wondered what the problem might be. He was healthy as an ox, never got a cold or the flu, and didn't have any allergies. He had barely aged a day since his early twenties. He was stronger than ten men and sharp-witted to near genius. What was wrong with him that he needed to go back and see the doctor?

An Asian woman with an electronic clipboard was waiting in the small blue examination room. There were furrows above her brow, and she looked anxious and nervous.

"Give it to me straight, Doc," Zion said, plopping down on the edge of the paper-covered exam table. He put his hands together and dropped them between his knees. "I'm healthy, for all intents and purposes. You're gonna tell me I got some type of tumor or something growing like a ticking time bomb in me? Something I haven't felt the effects of yet?"

"No." Her sharp, monosyllabic answer didn't make him feel any better. "Mr. Wilson, I want to take you through a series of tests, and I want you to perform them to the best of your ability. Do you understand?"

"Tests?" He didn't understand. He thought he was finished with tests.

"Follow me, please."

Zion was reluctant, but he followed the doctor with the long black hair that fell to the middle of her back. She had haunted eyes, circles underneath them as if she worked long hours with little rest. He had questions, and nobody seemed to have any answers. She led him down a long hallway to his right, the windows streaming bright sunlight. Zion peeked outside. A movement out of the corner of his eye caused him to glance back, and he noticed two men in black suits were a few paces behind him.

The doctor took Zion to the elevators, and the men followed them inside. They all went down.

"What are these tests about? Do I need to call my wife?"

"Mr. Wilson, we'd be happy to contact your wife for you," said one of the gentlemen.

Zion stepped back and pressed his spine against the cool metal wall of the elevator. With sweaty palms, he gripped the handrail that lined the wall. His eyebrows lifted, and creases wrinkled his forehead as he replied tensely, "Someone better tell me what the hell is going on here." He had visions of secret medical facilities, and the place was starting to look more and more like one.

The two men in suits barely glanced in his direction. One of them chuckled briefly. The doctor glared at them and glanced back at Zion. "I'm sorry, Mr. Wilson. I'm not authorized to tell you any more information until nondisclosure forms are—"

"I'm not signing no nondisclosure forms!" he said. Zion lurched forward and banged on the elevator doors. "Let me out of here!" he shouted. "I didn't sign up for this! Let me out!"

The gentlemen in black placed heavy hands on his shoulders and pulled him back. "Please, remain calm."

The elevator doors opened on the basement floor, and Zion Wilson shot out, tearing from their grasp. He looked to the left and to the right but didn't see any way out, so he blindly ran straight ahead.

"Mr. Wilson!" Dr. Yamazaki called after him. They would hurt him. She knew Meade's henchmen would have no qualms about taking down the patient if he didn't cooperate. "Mr. Wilson, please! For your safety, you have to stop!"

Zion dashed past a startled man in a lab coat, his wingtips slapping against the white linoleum floor. His suit jacket whipped out behind him, and his arms pumped as quickly as his legs. He didn't get winded. He coasted around a corner, and there ahead of him was a door labeled Exit. A burly security guard tried to stop him, but Zion pushed the man away with all his considerable strength. The oversized man flew six feet in the air and landed with a deafening crash through a glass wall of the laboratory. Zion knew he could get out. He just had to keep running.

"Stop!" Dr. Yamazaki pleaded.

One of the black-suited men leveled his weapon and fired the tranquilizer dart directly into the back of Zion's neck. The cartridge was double strength. The medium-height, medium-build runner didn't stand a chance.

Akiko covered her mouth and dropped her head. "You didn't have to do that!" she shouted. "Go get him!" She pointed at her patient and stormed to the laboratory. Within a few minutes, Zion was deposited on a stretcher in the basement examination room. Akiko's laboratory permitted a view from a level above. The room was sealed off by automated doors that opened only by access code.

"Who do we have here?" asked Yuhle. He strolled into her office, peering down at the patient.

"Zion Wilson, case number 6458004e. Our rapid results from the DNA sequencer indicated a probable match with the Atlantis gene. I received word this morning we're to run further tests and document phenotypic and behavioral abnormalities." Akiko heaved a sigh, finally catching her breath after chasing him. "Make a note that he's fast and strong."

"Are we safe?" Yuhle's hawkish nose twitched. He wasn't comfortable dealing with a potentially violent patient.

"Don't worry, Yuhle. Nothing hands-on."

General Meade had ways of getting what he wanted and people to carry out his dirty work. A careful combination of mind-altering drugs would make Zion Wilson docile enough to complete the rigorous physical and mental tests required to assess his capabilities. They tested his strength by measuring the force of his punch. He could throw a smart car across a football field. His intelligence measured off the charts.

Zion could also perform minor telekinesis, such as moving a spoon across a table. He could read thoughts with 84 percent accuracy. Zion Wilson was no ordinary human being, and he didn't have ordinary genetic material. It was all adding up for him to be the first real match. "This is the one," Akiko murmured with growing amazement as she glanced from her clipboard to the patient dazedly performing superhuman feats beyond the bulletproof glass. "My friend, you are seeing the Atlantis gene in action."

Yuhle whistled. "How the hell does he do this stuff?"

"Ancient Atlantean mythos supplies vibrational energy as the source of their unique power. In theory, I'm guessing they possibly have the ability to affect the electromagnetic spectrum." She shrugged. "Honestly, I don't have a clue. But what if we could get a better understanding of the genes that make this possible? Do you know what that would mean for us? We could modify faulty genetic material with improved Atlantean genes. We could effectively cure cystic fibrosis and Down syndrome."

Dr. Yuhle shook his head. He was frustrated with that gleam in Akiko's eyes. It was a hungry gleam. She was so stuck in her vision that she couldn't see how others might use the knowledge. "Think about it, Dr. Yamazaki. The US military is supplying us with a list of names of people like Zion Wilson, people who can read minds and throw cars. You might not think there's something strange about that, but I do. They want these people for a reason...and I'm betting it isn't to cure disease."

APRIL 11, 2016, SAN FRANCISCO, CALIFORNIA

1:45 PM

Jaxon stood in the middle of the greenhouse, knowing she wasn't supposed to be there, but she was unafraid. She needed an escape, and it was the only place on the expansive property where she knew no one would find her. They would most definitely be looking for her everywhere else.

She had been at Forever Welcome just under a month, and she was growing more familiar with her foes. Seventeen-year-old Lizzie Baptiste, the leader of the pack, was the worst of them. Then there were Lizzie's emulators, adoring fifteen-year-old fans Beth Sharpton and Delilah Griffith. In the four weeks since Jaxon had arrived, the three girls had taken every opportunity to stir up trouble and push her around, from sly taunts to meetings in the public restroom.

The craziest part of the scenario was Lizzie's reason for bothering her. Jaxon had discovered—after overhearing a dining hall conversation between Lizzie and crew—that the eldest of the group was infatuated with Dr. Hollis, of all people. Apparently, Lizzie had decided the psychiatrist's interest in Jaxon's assimilation into the school was too close a doctor–patient relationship for comfort. Dr. Hollis was sweet, and while Jaxon hadn't had much respect for psychiatrists in the past as she had for him, she certainly wasn't interested in him like that. She was in the awkward position of feeling she couldn't go to the one person who would likely squash all the nonsense.

Jax had refrained from solving the disputes physically, but she was running out of self-restraint. She wanted to punch something. As her sprinting heart rate slowed to a normal rhythm and her breathing grew calmer, she let the vital energy of the growing things surround her and soothe her frazzled nerves.

"They're idiots," she muttered to herself. She wanted to use foul language and more apropos descriptions of the Cretans at the main house that were driving her insane with their immaturity, but she had gradually stopped using profanity after being at Forever Welcome for several weeks. *Idiots* was an apt enough term. Dim-witted, ignorant, slow to learn. She was sick of them, but she had two years to deal with them or people like them.

The rest of the residents barely paid her any attention. There were nine of the twelve- to fifteen-year-olds and ten within her own age bracket. The younger kids had far fewer freedoms than the older ones, and she rarely saw them other than during class and in passing during morning group therapy. The age brackets ate at separate times and had separate downtimes. Of the ten sixteen- to eighteen-year-olds, Jaxon had only one other nuisance besides Lizzie.

Delaney Houston, the pimply faced sixteen-year-old, had a crush on her, displayed with characteristic elementary school aplomb. If she was eating alone, he made himself a pest. If she was walking alone, he made himself a pest. He called her names and said she smelled funny and generally made himself a *pest*, but Jax could deal with him. A healthy dose of ignoring him was enough, after the first few weeks, to cut his ego down to size. He pretty much left her alone.

Lizzie and her ilk were the ones who seemed to have nothing better to do than torment her. Just as Jax had suspected, the minute word got out that she was taking advanced placement classes—as she knew it inevitably would—Jaxon was deemed the geek, the nerd, the weirdo. She was picked on for her size and her figure. She was too skinny. She was too stuck-up. She was the shrink's pet.

"Ugh!" she growled. She hated it.

Jaxon sank to the mulch-covered floor and inhaled slowly and deeply. The greenhouse was inordinately warm, the heat of the afternoon sun intensified by the clear paneling of the glass framework. Perspiration beaded along her forehead and rolled down her dusty face. She licked it from the top of her lips. She smiled to herself, feeling more at peace and at ease in the lonely shed than she had since arriving—or since having her arrival fantasies dashed by the reality of Forever Welcome. The name was a misnomer. Those people didn't want her there.

The greenhouse was about the size of her bedroom, and the walls were lined with two shelves, one high and one low, each holding potted plants. A large table dominated the middle of the small space with just enough of a pathway to circle the room, and a wire trellis extended from the tabletop to the framework of the roof. She followed the narrow mesh wall of trellis up and up to where buckets hung overhead, suspended from a sprinkler system.

Plants were on every available surface, and clay pots were home to aloe, pothos, and ferns. Planters were filled with pink and yellow flowering plants, and scarlet orchids climbed stabilizing sticks. An odd assortment of citronella pots was isolated from the rest of the plants along the wall farthest from the door. Their black plastic containers were labeled, and one group of plants labeled "Control" wasn't as robust as the other.

Jaxon touched the chartreuse fronds. Like partial snowflakes, they branched off in rounded spikes, and the foliage gave off a lemony scent. The plants labeled "Praise" overflowed their plastic containers. The control plants had fewer leaves. She was curious to know what type of experiment was going on.

Jaxon dug a finger into the moist, loamy dirt. "What are you guys doing?" she murmured to the citronella. As she touched the earth, she again experienced the strange tingle she had felt the first day she stepped into the backyard. She felt it in her toes. Her skin seemed to spark with static, and she felt a rush of adrenaline. Then, right before her eyes, the plant began a rapid growth that stole her breath.

Jaxon stumbled back, alarmed. Mulch kicked up under her shifting feet as she hit the ground, landing on her rump. She looked up at the plant on the shelf and watched as it visibly stretched an inch taller, its leaves shaking subtly. "Okay, that wasn't supposed to happen." Her voice was breathless with amazement and fear.

There was no way to get around it with the evidence right before her eyes. Something Jaxon had known all along was becoming impossible to ignore—she was different. It was the reason the kids back at the residence, kids everywhere, gave her a hard time. She wasn't like other people. She was smarter, stronger, and... more powerful?

Her eyebrows lowered over her heavy-lidded eyes as she shook her head. "This is just what I need," she muttered to herself. "More reason to be the butt of everyone's joke." No one could find out. Like the fingerprints left in the table at the courtroom, like the fights she had won through sheer impossible strength, it had to be kept a secret, but another worrisome thought was beginning to take shape. Why? Why was she so different from everyone else? What was wrong with her?

Dr. Hollis ambled into the greenhouse intending to check on his plants, but when he saw Jaxon sprawled on the ground, he called out in alarm, "Jax! Are you all right? What on earth are you doing in here?" The psychiatrist bustled forward and helped her to her feet.

"I'm fine," she replied too hastily. "I was just out for a walk, and I found this place."

Anthony eyed her suspiciously and glanced at his watch. "No, Jaxon, you're supposed to be in your bedroom. I got word from Ms. Bhati you reported a headache, and she released you from class early. Hey, I'm no rocket scientist, but I don't think the walk up the stairs to your room led you out here. So... why don't you tell me what's going on, and let me see if I can help?"

She bit her lips and looked around, racking her brain for an excuse, but none was forthcoming. Jaxon sighed and threw her arms up in surrender. "Things are getting out of hand up at the house, and I just don't know where to go to get some peace," she wailed, suddenly tearing up. Jax dashed the hot tears from her face and covered her eyes, taking deep breaths. She shook her head, pissed off for breaking down. "Look, I'm trying to do everything right, but it's just not working. I'm scared I'm going to hurt somebody!"

"Whoa, whoa. Calm down. Nobody's going to hurt anybody, and nobody's going to get hurt. Take some deep breaths for me, and let's get that anger under control." Her vehemence threw him into protective mode. Anthony guided her to a clear edge of the lower shelf and let her rest her backside against the ledge. He studied her face intently, realizing Jaxon wasn't the type to blow up over trivia. Something serious had to be taking place, and whatever it was, neither his teachers nor he were being let in on the secret. "What exactly is going on?"

"I'm no snitch," she said fiercely.

Anthony fought the urge to roll his eyes. He sighed and perched beside her. He let the silence clear the air between them. When she was ready to talk about it, she'd talk. "This is where I go when I need quiet time and space, too, so I don't blame you," he said.

Jaxon peeked at him out of the corner of her eye. "Is all this yours?"

"No, I wish I could claim credit for it all, but it isn't. Most of the flowers belong to Ms. Faye, the housekeeper. She likes gardening. The rest are waiting for the groundskeeper to plant them. That little grouping of citronella over there is mine, though." Anthony's roving eyes moved over his plants, and he sat up with interest. He pushed away from the shelf and strolled over to get a closer look. "Wow, look at that. This one has made a big leap since the last time I checked these little guys."

"R-really?" Jaxon said in a shaky voice. "How do you know? I bet it's just your imagination. Um, I mean, it looks the same to me."

"How would you know?" He grinned at the plant, eyeing the fronds, fingering the pot, and turning it around for a different perspective. It had definitely grown. Anthony dug a tailor's tape measure from the pocket of his wool slacks and held it against the plant. "Wow," he said. "A whole inch?" He peered at the label again. It was one of the controls. Anthony dropped his head in disappointment. His experiment had failed, and the controls were catching up to the Praise plants. "Oh, well. I guess that's that."

Jaxon cautiously tiptoed closer. "What's what?"

"Hmm? Oh, I was testing a hypothesis of mine, but it appears I was wrong and... science might be right. I, uh, I follow the works of a researcher named Emoto who posited that exposure to positive images could change the molecular structure of water. What I did was treat the water for the Praise plants with positive reinforcements, a daily prayer of thanksgiving for its benefits. I know. Sounds crazy." He grinned sheepishly.

"Not really." She shrugged. She could understand the psychiatrist subscribing to such a thought process, although it didn't sound all that scientific to her.

"Anyway, at first my Praise plants were outpacing the controls, but now it looks like they're catching up, more than likely negating any difference between the Praise and controls. At some point I'm going to have to stop chasing dreams. I mean, I don't have any hopes this stuff will make it into a journal or anything, but I was just curious, I guess."

Jaxon twisted her lips. "Maybe not. Maybe you need to keep going. That one could be a fluke." She reached for one of the citronella pots, careful not to touch the plant itself.

"You might be right, but I don't want to get my hopes up. Hey, what do you know about gardening?" Dr. Hollis asked. Gardening might be a great way to get her out of the house and away from whatever was bothering her.

"I've never done it before. I might have a green thumb." She tucked her hands in her pockets. She might have more than a green thumb. She might have some weird, freakish powers that caused plants to grow an inch at the touch of her hand. Jax rethought her first response. "Or not," she replied hurriedly. Knowing Dr. Hollis, he would try to assign her to the greenhouse permanently. "You know what? I'd probably kill everything. You'd better not let me near them."

Anthony burst out laughing and shook his head. "What if I told you that you could spend some time in here every evening? I'll get Mercado, the grounds-keeper, to pull together some resources for you. You can have your own pots, soil, seeds. Of course, you'll have to use some of your own funds to keep it up, but we'll start you off. Does that sound cool?"

She had to admit, it did. If she got out to the greenhouse every evening, she wouldn't have to put up with Lizzie's meanness after class. Between five in the evening and nine at night when it was time for lights out, Jaxon had been confining herself to her room to avoid conflicts. Even if she didn't touch a single seed or flowerpot, she could go out there and play on her phone or listen to her music.

A slow smile split across her face. "That would be fantastic," she said. "When can I start?"

Chapter 7

APRIL 11, 2016, ALBUQUERQUE,
NEW MEXICO

2:00 PM

Akiko used the access codes Yuhle
had given her. He had to heavily flirt
with a superior in order to get them. The
sealed doors hissed open like the maw
of a monster. Her assistant had confis-
cated the passwords to the only door in
the basement where Akiko and her crew
didn't have permission to go. She crept
through the opening. Her shallow breaths
sounded loud to her ears, but she tried

to move without making a sound. It was so cold in the room that each exhalation puffed before her face. She squeezed her arms around her slender torso and fought the chill, wondering why the basement freezer needed to be used in the research portion of the Poseidon Project.

Two security cameras were in upper corners of the room, but she knew to remain in the blind spot, and Akiko was sure she was beyond their range. The bulbs recessed in the ceiling dropped intense white light upon the slick, reflective linoleum and bounced off walls lined with chrome drawers. She had seen drawers like that before—they were freezers to hold the deceased.

"Why would they be holding on to the dead?" she said to herself. Akiko studied the printed labels on the drawer closest to her. Wilson, Zion—she recognized the name. "Oh no," she whispered in shock. He was one of the patients who had tested positive for the Atlantis gene. When she had last seen the thirty-two-year-old man with the glacial-blue eyes and sable-brown skin, he was alive and well. "What have they done to you?"

Akiko had spent the better part of two months working with Yuhle and the team provided by General Meade, going through the thousands of names on the ever-growing list, and in all that time, she had found only six matches. She counted the labeled drawers—counted all six. Her heart hammered into her throat.

She eased open Zion's drawer a fraction. The soft squeal of metal against metal made her stop. She could see the body within, but it wasn't as she had feared. He didn't appear to be dead. Akiko stood on her tiptoes and stared down at Zion, wondering about the attachments, the wires and electrodes tacked to his temples, scalp, and chest. She noticed the slow rise and fall as he breathed. No, he wasn't dead, but he wasn't just sleeping. He appeared comatose. She swallowed thickly and shut the drawer.

Her lips firmed in a straight, hard line. She could no longer ignore the obvious. Yuhle was right. General Meade was up to something terrible, and he was making her an accomplice in his dark deeds. Something had to be done, but what? Tears welled up in her heavy-lidded eyes, and she sniffed, trying to suppress the sound. The place was so silent, the quietest intake of air had hurricane force. Akiko shook her head vehemently. Her time with the facility was up. She had to get away from the place.

She crept a little deeper into the room, hoping to see as much as she could from her vantage point without being caught on camera. The rest of the empty freezer drawers stretched along the wall before giving way to an open area where six sealed vats stood, gauzy creatures floating within, all in various stages of development. Akiko covered her mouth in horror. What were those creatures, and what were they doing there?

She braved the cameras. Akiko tiptoed forward. The vats were transparent cylinders the height of a man, and the creatures were enmeshed in a gossamer, membranous substance submerged in clear fluid. Akiko squinted her eyes. She saw legs, hands, and misshapen skulls. Some were embryos of some sort, but they weren't entirely human—they were a hybrid species. Their skin was translucent, and their veins were throbbing beneath. Their hair was pale white or silver. Their limbs were longer and skinnier than those of humans. They were smaller. The largest of the creatures looked like an undersized adult and stretched its placenta in a languid sweep of arms and legs as it turned to face Akiko, almost as if it sensed her presence.

Akiko's heart throbbed. The rumors were true. There was something sinister going on at the research and development center, and she was disappointed to realize she was a part of it, but she determined to find out everything necessary to shut the place down. The adult creature opened its eyes and "saw" her.

Akiko stumbled back, shaken to her core. She had to get out, but she had legal obligations there. She couldn't just walk out of the building and run to the nearest reporter and spill her guts. She had to act wisely. The more she knew and the more she learned about the Poseidon Project's true purpose, the more leverage she would have. Akiko reached into the side of her pants where she had duct taped the small, thin cell phone she snuck past Starke's security team earlier in the day.

With trembling hands, she held up the phone and started snapping pictures. She photographed the humanoid hybrid creatures floating in the vats. She photographed the rows and rows of drawers, most of them unlabeled but a few with bodies housing the undead, the comatose—for what reason, she had no clue.

She took as many pictures as she could in the few minutes she dared linger. Then, she raced from the room and scurried up the hall, away from the scene of her break-in. She hurried to her office and didn't stop briskly walking until she was safely behind the glass doors with Yuhle. He looked up from his computer, his gray eyes solemn. "Did you do it?" he whispered, his lips barely moving.

Akiko nodded. "After work. Meet me at the coffee shop." An employee in a lab coat walked past the window and glanced in, and Akiko jumped, clutching her chest. "Yuhle, we have to get out of here. I don't know how, but we have to."

Yuhle hopped up from his desk and tucked his arm around his mentor. "Listen to me. We will. Okay? I'll get us out of here. Just... we have to do what we have to, to stay under the radar. Do you understand?"

She cried, nodding her head and burying her face in Yuhle's neck. "What have I gotten us into?"

APRIL 11, 2016, SAN FRANCISCO, CALIFORNIA

5:35 PM

"You're starting to become a bore, dogface," Lizzie hissed menacingly.

Jaxon looked up from her magazine, startled by the sound of her nemesis behind her. She whipped around in the overstuffed armchair and glared. "Didn't I tell you to stay away from me? Lizzie, this is getting old." Her nails dug crescents into her palms as she balled her fists. A quick glance around showed her they were alone in the great room.

Lizzie sneered, her coral-red lips twisting over the mouthful of metal. With a different attitude, she would be a pretty girl. Her auburn hair flowed around her face in feathery layers that accentuated the slant of her cheeks. Her large, doe-like eyes were squeezed in a scowl. She looked Jaxon up and down.

"He's just not that into you, girl. Why don't you stop making yourself look easy? If you throw yourself at Anthony any harder, you'll break something."

Jaxon rose to her full height, a little under five feet. Her eyes were at Lizzie's mouth level. "If you're that desperate for attention from him, then why don't you stop yapping and throw the first punch."

"You think I won't?" Lizzie took a threatening step forward, rage written plainly on her face. She was fed up with what she thought were Jaxon's attempts at stealing her crush. The girl was delusional. Dr. Hollis was far too mature to get tangled up with a foolish teenage girl. Jaxon suppressed a sigh and refrained from once again stating the obvious.

"You're not worth the FW points," she said, shaking her head. Jaxon grabbed her magazine to leave the great room. Class time had ended an hour ago, and most of the other residents were wrapped up in extracurricular activities. Soon enough, Jaxon would have something to do in the evenings, too, once Dr. Hollis made arrangements for her to get in the greenhouse, but until then, she planned to avoid the girl who just couldn't seem to leave her alone.

Lizzie grabbed her shoulder and snatched her around to face her. Jaxon angrily chopped her wrist and broke the painful grip. Lizzie was taller and bigger than she was, but she wasn't intimidated. "That was your last warning," Jaxon growled.

"I saw you out in the greenhouse with him. You were supposed to be in your room. Wait until everyone hears what a slu—"

"Problem, ladies?"

The boys' resident assistant saved Lizzie from getting her braces prematurely readjusted. Both girls turned to the entry archway where Otto Heike casually peered into the room. The athletic eighteen-year-old had his arms lifted, fingers hooked in the molding of the arch. His muscular torso was elongated, and his white T-shirt stretched taut against his sweaty chest. His piercing gray eyes darted from Lizzie's face to Jaxon's as he swung back and forth on the tips of his toes. He dropped to the floor and crossed his arms.

Dr. Hollis had pulled him aside during lunch. He had asked Otto to keep an eye on the new student and find out who was giving her a hard time. His lips curved upward in one corner. It didn't take much looking around to see that the resident mean girl was involved.

Lizzie pasted on a sweet smile and clasped her hands behind her back. "Not at all, Otto. We were just having a friendly girl chat. I'm keeping the newbie in line." She threw an arm around Jaxon and dragged her close. Jaxon shook off the arm and stepped away.

Otto's dark brows lowered over his watchful eyes. "Thanks, Lizzie. But Loren is the girls' RA. If there's anything Jaxon needs to know, you can direct her to Lo next time. And aren't you supposed to be with the art class out on the patio for your extracurricular?" Lizzie sulked, her full lips pouty. Otto pointed to the door, and Lizzie stamped from the room, leaving Jaxon to face him alone.

She had seen the authoritative youth around the residence during the three and a half weeks she had been there, but she'd never had reason to speak with him. Seeing him up close and personal, she realized why half the girls at Forever Welcome considered Otto Heike the hottest boy on campus.

He had sun-kissed brown hair with deep copper natural highlights, a tousled array of wayward curls spilling across his forehead. He had a sharp, straight nose above a sensually carved mouth. Jaxon hitched in a breath as she studied his strikingly handsome face. He had a square chin and the slightest dark brown fuzz of a beard.

He wore a T-shirt and gym shorts since his extracurricular was the fitness team. In the basement of Forever Welcome was a makeshift gym packed with hand-me-down fitness equipment, and Otto and a few friends pumped iron and slap boxed after classes. He looked the pipsqueak up and down. He had seen her around but never really paid her any attention. Jaxon Andersen kept to herself.

His smoke-gray eyes searched her face to make sure she was okay. She looked mad as a rattlesnake in a box, but she didn't appear too shaken up. "What's your extracurricular?" he asked.

"I don't have one yet."

"Oh, really? You want to come downstairs and hang out with my crew? We do some weightlifting, stuff like that. I mean, you don't have to do anything. Just to get you out of the target zone. I know how Lizzie can be. She likes to give the new girls trouble, but she's all talk, harmless."

"Yeah, I figured." Jaxon sighed. She crossed her arms, trying to tamp down her oversized temper. "You said you guys lift weights?"

He lifted and dropped his shoulders. "We got ellipticals and a stationary bike, too. Yoga mats. All that crap is collecting dust. You can bust it out. Come on. Let me show you." He waved her over, a smile on his lips. She looked as if she was trying to come up with an excuse to turn him down, but Otto wasn't having that. Jaxon Andersen wasn't the type to invite a second glance, but if someone did look twice, they'd see something that made it hard to look away. The more Otto stared at her, the more he wanted to get to know her.

Besides, she was little. He had heard she was sixteen, but she looked closer to twelve. Maybe she could use some toughening up, and working out with the fitness group would help her gain some confidence.

He jogged into the foyer, and she dragged her feet, but she followed. She hadn't been in the basement, though she had seen nearly all the other main areas of the house. She enjoyed the game room upstairs, which was equipped with video game consoles, laptops, and flat screens. Like the attic, the basement had an open, airy floor plan and bright walls to give the illusion of spaciousness. She trudged down the stairs in Otto's wake and peeked in down below. They stepped down on the foam-covered floor.

There were three elliptical exercise machines and a stationary bike, with teens of all ages using the equipment and chatting companionably as they worked out. The atmosphere was more relaxed than she would've imagined. They looked as if they were having fun. There were weight benches, and free weights were stacked on a shelf beside a floor-to-ceiling mirror. Most of the older guys were using them. A section of floor was squared off and covered with yoga mats that weren't getting much use.

Jaxon's gaze went straight to the boxing bag standing in a corner where a ponytailed blonde was throwing hard blows against the battered, beaten leather. A smile lit Jaxon's face. "This place is awesome," she gushed.

Otto nodded, surprised it was her speed. "You like it? Get in where you fit in. I can help you put together a routine right quick if you want to. Was thinking maybe you wanted to run through some self-defense maneuvers... bet you get picked on a lot for being so little." His voice had a teasing lilt, and he tugged playfully at a strand of her jet-black hair.

Jaxon swatted away his hand, grinning. "I can handle myself, trust me."

Otto bounced around on his toes, hands up. He threw a few feints, which she easily avoided. "Uh-oh, you look like you got some moves. Hang on. I got mitts." He led her over to the boxing area and put mitts on his hands to let her practice some punches.

Jaxon blushed, laughing. She covered her face and shook her head. "Challenge!" The blonde, Loren, pulled off the boxing gloves and handed them to her. "Nice to see you finally mingling, Jax."

Jax wrinkled her nose with a tight, nervous smile. They weren't letting her refuse. Delaney, the pest, spoke up for her. "I bet she can put you on your ass, Otto." She grinned, looking around in surprise at the crowd that was gathering. It was weird. They weren't taunting her or picking on her or cheering for somebody to beat her up. They were rallying around her. It was almost as if she was a part of the fun instead of the butt of a joke.

"Okay," she said uncertainly.

She put on the boxing gloves and punched out with her right hand. Jaxon allowed her wrist to weakly curve downward. She didn't want to hit him with her full force. Jax was well aware she could knock the buff Otto Heike into tomorrow. She would have to pull her punches.

"That was pretty good. Put a little more power behind it," he coaxed.

Loren stepped up behind her and positioned her arms correctly. "It's all about form. Ever been in a fight before?" Jaxon shrugged. The residents didn't know her history just as she didn't know theirs. It was considered impolite at Forever Welcome to pry into another person's background. Loren put a hand beneath Jaxon's spaghetti arms and thrust them up so her fists were at face level. Lo kicked Jaxon's feet so she would spread her legs a little wider. "Stay nimble," she directed.

"Hit him, Jax!" Delaney cheered for her.

Jaxon bit her lip and punched a little harder. Otto backed up a step with the blow. "Dang, girl! That's a mean right hook." Otto chuckled, holding up his mitts and beckoning for her to come again. She took a few more swings, keeping the force behind the punches at the same intensity or a little less.

"All right, all right!" Jaxon feigned breathlessly and pulled off the gloves. "Let someone else go."

She was smiling as she stepped back to root for the next person. She was amazed and in disbelief—they wanted to hang out with her. The boxing practice went on for another hour until the participants drifted off to other pursuits in the gym, and Jaxon studied her options. She moved around to an elliptical and stepped up, noticing that signs on each piece of equipment let residents know what age level the machines served.

"Look at me, Jaxon!" a thirteen-year-old boy on the stationary bike called out. "Want me to show you how fast I can ride?"

Otto strolled past the kid and ruffled his straight brown hair. "Show off, Hinkly," he said with a laugh.

"I'm not a show-off," Hinkly protested. "I just want to talk to her, that's all."

Jaxon giggled as Otto made his way to her side and hopped on the elliptical next to her. "Look out, Jaxon. I think you have a secret admirer," he whispered dramatically. Jaxon blushed and waved playfully at the kid. She set the pace on her machine to match Otto's. "Hinkly wants to know if you have a boyfriend."

Jaxon gave Otto a sideways glance. "Does Hinkly want to know or does someone else want to know?" Was he flirting with her?

Otto pumped his arms up and down, staring straight ahead, as he walked on the machine. "Inquiring minds want to know."

"No, I don't have a boyfriend." She ducked her head to hide her grin and kept walking. "Do either of the RAs have a significant other?" There were only two, one for the boys and one for the girls, and she wanted to know the answer for only one of them. She wasn't bold enough to ask Otto outright, though.

"One of them does," he answered.

She asked, "Which one?"

"Not me, obviously," he said, chuckling. "If I did, my girlfriend would definitely be jealous about me talking to a beautiful woman like you."

Their eyes connected, and his magnetism was impossible to miss. She couldn't drag her gaze away. Otto licked his lips and bit the bottom one, and Jaxon followed the swipe of his tongue with her eyes. She chuckled nervously.

Later in the night, she lay awake in bed, staring at the ceiling and thinking about the boy with the smoke-gray eyes. She'd never really been interested in a guy before, probably because she was rarely in one place for long. She closed her eyes, wondering what tomorrow would bring. She had been at the group home for nearly a month, and she was starting to feel as if she fit in somewhere. The evening was proof, wasn't it? The same kids she had avoided getting to know had accepted her. Sure, there were Lizzie and her cohorts to deal with, but Jaxon was determined to make the best of her two-year sentence... especially if it meant she had more time to get to know Otto Heike.

Chapter 8

APRIL 11, 2016, ALBUQUERQUE,
NEW MEXICO

7:00 PM

They met after work, in a coffee shop on the other side of the unfamiliar city. Akiko had a condominium lease as part of her agreement to work on the project. She chose a meeting location as far away from home as possible.

The night was starless. The city streets were nearly empty as she drove her white BMW, guided by her GPS. She parallel parked and looked up to see Yuhle waiting for her by the coffee shop entrance. A baseball cap covered his sandy-brown hair, and he wore blue jeans. It was odd to see him out of his lab coat. He looked like anybody—or nobody.

Akiko turned off the engine and tried to shake the sense of impending doom. Meade could have someone tailing her just to keep an eye on what she was doing away from the research facility. She knew he worked with the NSA. He could have her phone tapped or her emails under surveillance. She felt scrutinized and in danger, but she couldn't help that. She had made a deal with the devil, and it came with the contract.

"And even if they're watching," she mumbled to herself, "is it a crime to meet with a friend? I have to act naturally." She mustered her courage and climbed out. She hit the remote control to lock the doors and set the alarm and hurried up to Yuhle. Akiko had a soft smile on her thin lips and swiped her hair out of her face, trying to appear normal.

"I thought you weren't going to show."

"I couldn't call you. It's not safe," she said. "Come on inside."

He followed her into the dimly lit interior of the coffee shop where the amber lighting gave the illusion of intimacy. The yellow ocher walls were warm and inviting. One wall of the room boasted floor-to-ceiling bookshelves, and a comfortable faded green sofa was catty-corner near the front of the coffee shop, a teenage girl curled up with a book. It was nearing seven o'clock, and there weren't many patrons.

The duo nervously made their way to the counter where Akiko ordered chai latte while Yuhle opted for a macchiato. They waited wordlessly for their orders to be filled. When the cups hit the counter-top, the weary scientists grabbed them gratefully and hurried to a table near the back of the coffee shop so Akiko could watch the door.

"I know what I must do, and you're not going to like it, but I have to do it. I need to get closer to the general." She said the last over Yuhle's protests. "He's the only one who can tell us what he's doing."

"No, no, Akiko. I've thought this through. Tomorrow morning, you need to give them your resignation, and I'll give them mine."

"We can't. We need to keep going as we are. It's the only way."

He slammed the coffee cup down on the table and yanked off his baseball cap. Yuhle ran his shaking fingers through his hair, considering her suggestion and quickly discarding it with a shake of his head. "What we need to do is cut ties, okay? They don't own us. We're under no obligation to continue to take part in this."

"Think about what you're saying, Yuhle. Do you really think General Meade is just going to let me walk away from everything?" She kept her voice level and low. There was no point in attracting anyone's attention. Akiko glanced around the nearly empty shop to see who might be eavesdropping.

Yuhle huffed, chest heaving. She was right. Everyone knew Dr. Yamazaki was a priceless asset. No one else had the Atlantis gene copy to compare with the test subjects, and no one else understood the research process well enough to get accurate results. The general would probably resort to keeping her around by any means necessary—even against her will.

"At least if I cozy up to him, he won't suspect I'm working against him. Which brings me to the next part of the process. I'm going to start keeping two sets of files. The official reports we send to them will make it seem like we're having trouble finding more matches. We can't let any more people fall victim to what happened to Zion."

Akiko rifled through her oversized handbag and dug out her cell phone. She had already printed the pictures and made digital copies, and she would erase the device as soon as Yuhle had a look. She slid the phone across the table. His eyes looked haunted by what he saw. Yuhle put a hand to his mouth as he scrolled through image after image, the color leaving his face.

"This is unnatural," he replied. Akiko nodded. "What do we do now?" he asked in a hoarse, uncertain voice.

"We do exactly as you originally suggested. We stay under the radar. We keep our noses clean, and most importantly, we make them believe whatever they need to believe to be able to trust us. Then, and only then, will we gain access to the information we need to make sure this project never, ever goes any further than it's already gone."

APRIL 12, 2016, SAN FRANCISCO, CALIFORNIA

9:45 AM

Jaxon was unable to keep up her charade.

She noticed him—Otto Heike—no matter how many times she looked away when he looked in her direction or how many times she pretended to be too preoccupied to pay attention to him. When she went to group therapy and listened as the other sixteen- to eighteen-year-olds chatted about their plans for the weekend, she couldn't take her eyes off him. Breakfast wasn't any better. For a second, he had looked as if he wanted to join her at the lonely table outside and away from everybody else where she crept to eat, but his friend, Lewis, had called his name, and Otto had sat with his regulars.

By the time she made it to class the day after her stint with Otto's fitness group, there was no getting around it—she liked him. It was… different. The near brush with him in the dining hall at breakfast had left her frazzled and breathless. She had butterflies, tingly hands, and sweaty palms. Was that what it was like to like someone? She had never really liked a guy in that way. The word *boyfriend* tumbled around in her thoughts like a foreign word.

She fidgeted through class, struggling to maintain focus. Her grades at Forever Welcome were superb, according to her monthly progress report. "Get it together, Jaxon," she admonished herself, reaching for the mouse and powering through another lesson. If she wanted to improve the B she had gotten in English Lit, she couldn't spend the morning daydreaming about Otto. She banned him from her thoughts and finished her assignments.

Lunch time arrived, and Jaxon hurried out of class to steer clear of Lizzie but also to avoid Otto. She had no clue what to say to him. She caught his eye as she passed his cubicle and quickly ducked her head, blushing. "Where you runnin' off to, dogface?" Lizzie called after her in the hallway, snickering. Jaxon ignored her and shoved open the dining hall doors.

She swiped her ID to clock in for lunch, taking her place in the line of students fixing plates at the buffet longboard, and as soon as she had what she wanted, Jax ducked through the stained-glass door to the patio. She sat at her table to eat in pleasant solitude. She was just about to congratulate herself for getting out without hassle when Otto dropped his tray on her table and plopped down with a friendly greeting on the bench across from her.

"What are you doing?" she asked. Her arctic eyes slid from his tray to his face. He was insanely cute. That face had haunted her dreams the night before and had been an obstacle in class. His square chin and angular cheeks, his hooded gray eyes and his lips—sweet mercy. Guys like that didn't eat lunch with girls like her. She was average, barely even noticeable. Why was he suddenly so interested in her?

With dancing, mischievous eyes, he gestured to his food with his fork and knife. "What does it look like I'm doing?"

"No, I mean you always eat inside with everybody else. What are you doing out here?"

"I'm out here because…" He smiled and took a bite, chewed thoughtfully, and gazed off in the distance before giving her a focused stare. "I want to get to know you."

She pushed back her plate, too nervous to eat. "There isn't really anything to get to know."

Otto wagged a finger at her. "Oh, yeah, there is. There's something about you. I can't put my finger on it, but you're not like other girls."

Jax squinted her eyes. He was right about that. He just didn't know how right he was. She sighed, smiling. He was making it impossible for her to ignore him, avoid him, pretend he didn't exist, and all of that was hard enough without him flirting with her. "I bet you say that to all the girls."

"Yeah, you're right. But it usually works. I must be losing my touch," he said playfully. Jax grabbed a napkin, crumpled it, and threw it at him, and Otto erupted with laughter. "But seriously… I've been here for a year, going on two. I have a year and a half to go. In all the time I've been here, I haven't met anyone who has captivated my attention quite the way you do. That's not a line, either."

"It sounds like a line," she teased.

"Well, can you blame me? I gotta pull out all the stops to get you to notice me. You go out of your way to avoid people. You antisocial or something?" he said, eyebrow raised. "'Cause you make getting close to you about as easy as bear-hugging a cactus." He chuckled dryly, sending butterflies through her core.

Jaxon shrugged and brushed her shoulder-length black hair out of her honey-brown face. "In my experience, sticking to myself is the easiest way to stay out of trouble. I've got two years in here, plus probation. I don't want more time added onto me 'cause somebody decides to be a jerk and set me off. So, I do what I have to do to limit my contact with others. Like, if I had a warning label, it would say *volatile*." She chuckled, and he grinned at her.

"Ooh, should I stay back? Nah, you look harmless," he said. His eyes crinkled with amusement as his gaze slowly trailed over her. Otto Heike liked what he saw.

"Don't make me show you," she warned.

"Show me what?" He dropped his voice intimately. He reached across the table and caressed her with a knuckle that brushed feather-light down the slant of her honeyed face. The unexpected skin-to-skin contact made Jaxon's almond-shaped eyes widen and her mouth drop open. Color splotched the apples of her cheeks, and Jaxon leaned closer, spell-bound. "The real you or the facade, Jaxon Andersen, 'cause I got a feeling there's more to you than meets the eye. Am I right? You stick to yourself because you don't want anybody to set you off, yet to me, that says you have a vulnerable side, so you kick up a defense to hide your weakness."

She sat back, frowning. "I'm not weak," Jax countered. She wasn't sure she liked his phrasing, and his touch was distracting and probably a tad bit inappropriate. She shook off the disorientation that came from close contact with Otto. She hoped he wasn't trying to put her down with a backward compliment. It would suck to have to instantly dislike him.

Otto waved off her response. "Everybody has a weakness, even me. I didn't mean to offend you, though. I'm not saying you're weak. I'm saying I find it alluring that there is a vulnerability to you as well as a fierceness. I'm curious to know why you're here."

"I thought it was rude to ask people questions like that. Come to think of it, I never hear anybody asking anybody else that, but two or three people have already asked me. See, that's what I'm talking about. What, I don't look like I have the balls to do something that will get me in trouble? I look too scrawny?" She was getting angry, and she didn't understand why. It was obvious Otto was just trying to talk to her, but it felt like a personal attack. "I get this everywhere I go," she whispered. "That's why I'm here."

Jaxon got up from the table to leave, but Otto reached out and caught her by the wrist. He stared up at her with his smoky eyes, and Jaxon was arrested by his gaze and the heat of his palm against her lower arm. She stopped.

"You don't have to run off. If anybody should leave, it's me. This is your table, and I'm sorry for getting you upset. But to be honest, all I want to do is sit out here in the sun with you and have a friendly conversation. Is that all right? I would love to get to know you better, but that's on your terms. Look, you don't have to talk about anything you don't want to talk about with me."

She reluctantly resumed her seat. Otto chuckled. "Boy, do you have a temper on you." He threw his hands up apologetically when she looked as if she wanted to protest. "Hey, no judgment from me. And by the way, the reason you probably never hear anybody else asking why the other residents are here is that most of us arrived long before you came. Everybody knows everybody's backstory but yours. Now, me? I have a thing for lighting fires."

"What?" Jaxon peered at him, surprised and not sure she believed his confession. "No way."

Otto Heike seemed like one of the most responsible, mature people on the grounds. He was the resident assistant for the boys' side of the dormitory floor, and he was entrusted with maintaining order when teachers or other staff were unavailable. He didn't look like a problem kid. On the other hand, Jaxon realized she was judging a book by its cover, the same thing she hated people doing to her. Everybody in Forever Welcome was there because of behavioral problems back home. She looked at Otto with new eyes.

"I'm in here for arson," he continued. "Ever since I was a little kid, I had an infatuation with the way a fire could slowly and beautifully wreak havoc. It started with small things like playing with matches or building little bonfires in the field behind my parents' house. I didn't get caught until I burned down an abandoned barn on my neighbor's property. They pressed charges. Apparently, they had some antiques or something like that in there. I had to pay restitution and everything."

"Wow, that's crazy," she said in awe.

"It was crazy. After the fact, I thought about what could have happened if the fire had gotten out of control. What if a spark would've made its way to my house or even to the neighbors' houses? People could've gotten hurt. I made some messed-up choices, and I'm still struggling with the urge to light. I just really like to see a nice fire burn, you know?"

His expression was wistful, as if he missed the smell of smoke and the heat of the flames.

Another fire was being tended at the table. Jaxon was awash in hormones, her interest impossible to hide. The faint hint of his cologne wafted to her nose. She studied his intense eyes, the lower lids as full as the top, giving him a bedroom-eyes stare. His lips curved upward in the left corner as he studied her just as closely. Jaxon suddenly wondered what it would be like to kiss those lips.

"Uh, we don't want to be late back to class." Jaxon shook herself out of her reverie.

"You barely touched your food," he pointed out.

"I don't eat much," she said.

Otto grabbed a French fry off her plate and bit it. "We've still got fifteen minutes until lunch is over. But if you're ready to leave, I'll walk you back, if you'd like."

She felt unsettled. He wouldn't break eye contact, which made it hard for her to think. Jaxon opened her mouth to speak but forgot what she was about to say. She colored in embarrassment. Both Jaxon and Otto started to laugh.

Then, the sound of a throat clearing from the vicinity of the dining hall door got their attention. "Hi there, Otto," Dr. Hollis said with a wave. He pushed up his glasses and took in the patio tableau, the teenagers wrapped up in conversation, and he felt a sense of accomplishment at crossing another hurdle with Jax, in a roundabout way. He had sent Otto to make sure no one was giving her a hard time, but it looked as if the two were hitting it off. "Jaxon, I just wanted to tell you the garden supplies are out at the greenhouse. So if you want to start this evening, you can."

"Oh, thanks," Jaxon replied. She sat up straighter in her chair and tried to look expressionless. She could tell the psychiatrist thought something was going on between her and Otto by the knowing look on his face. She smiled to herself when he ducked back into the dining hall. The question was, was there something going on between them?

"You're working in the greenhouse?" Otto asked.

"Yeah, it's my new extracurricular."

Otto thrust his lower lip forward and crossed his arms like a petulant five-year-old. "I totally thought I'd won you over to the fitness group. You didn't enjoy yourself yesterday? You looked like you were having a good time."

Jaxon smiled. She had had a good time. Had she known about the fitness group before finding out about the greenhouse, she would've chosen it. "Maybe I can do both," she suggested.

"I was thinking I could show you some self-defense moves, build up your confidence. If you want to do both, though, that's even better. I show you some tricks, and you can show me some. I have to warn you, though. Every plant I've ever touched has died a slow, painful death."

Jaxon giggled. "Slow and painful?" she asked. Otto nodded solemnly.

"It's true. My mom took a cutting from one of those hanging houseplants and told me it would grow if I put it in a cup with water. Needless to say, it lasted a whopping three days before giving up the ghost."

She doubled over, laughing harder. "Otto!"

"You'd be doing me a great service to teach me how not to kill flowers. A disservice to the plants, maybe."

They rose from the table and grabbed their trays. He walked her back to class, and for the first time, Jaxon didn't have to worry about anyone's taunts or dirty looks. Loren and some of the others from the fitness group chatted with her before class was back in session. Her sense of belonging resurged.

Chapter 9

APRIL 13, 2016, SAN FRANCISCO,
CALIFORNIA

3:30 PM

Jaxon slipped away from the main house at three thirty when classes were over to spend the hours set aside for extracurricular activities in the greenhouse. She had been reluctant to try what she was about to try, but she couldn't get the idea out of her head. She hurried under the archway from the backyard to the secret garden. Wisteria blossoms trailed and dropped fragrant, feathery flowers in her hair. She passed the flowing fountain. She skirted the tidy rows of apple trees alive with the buzz of bumblebees, and she came upon the greenhouse at the back of the yard.

The building was small, only eight by six feet, its steel framework painted rust red with stabilized frosted-fiberglass walls and rooftop. From the outside, she could see the contours of plants. The door was unlocked, as it had been before, and when she walked into the much warmer room, she instantly started to sweat. Jax inhaled, feeling the tingle of awareness and the rich connection with the dirt beneath the mulch. The sensation of an unseen energy moving between her and the earth had only gotten stronger with her time at Forever Welcome, which she attributed to the group home's verdant, vibrant gardens and landscape. But Jax wasn't in the greenhouse to escape with her thoughts—she was there to experiment with the potting soil and seeds Dr. Hollis had procured for her.

On the back shelf where Dr. Hollis kept his plants, the citronella she had touched days before had grown another three inches, leaves spilling over the sides of the pot and a yellow flower blooming from a stalk near its center. Jaxon made a beeline for the grouping of mosquito plants and studied them in awe. "Unbelievable," she murmured. She had done that. She had the power to do things like that. It was stunning and somewhat terrifying. She wondered what else she could do.

Jaxon didn't know a thing about planting, but on the table in the middle of the cozy greenhouse were a bag of potting soil, several small earthen pots, and a tiny rake and trowel. She was out of her element, but she pushed up the sleeves of her denim shirt. Her hair was tied back with a silk scarf. She tore a tiny hole in the potting soil bag and scooped some of the rich, black dirt into each pot.

"All right. That looks about right." Jax put her hands on her hips to survey the handiwork. There were crumbs of soil littering the table and spilling from the overfilled pots, but it didn't look too bad. She set about opening each packet of seeds she had requested and poked them down into the soil. Jax had asked for herbs because she'd read somewhere they were easy to cultivate. She wasn't sure how deeply the seeds needed to be planted. She didn't know how much water they required or which fertilizer to add. Jax moved instinctively.

As she moved from the first pot to the second, she hummed a tuneless melody. She felt the tingle of awareness that was always strongest in the garden, and she sank into a relaxed, thoughtless zone. Gradually, she became aware of a change in what was happening in her hands. The minute her fingers touched the seeds, they started to sprout. Jax stared at them. "Is this supposed to happen?" She hurriedly buried them in the dirt. Right before her eyes, lavender shoots pushed through the soil and stretched toward her body as if she were the sun.

Her eyes flew to the first pot she had planted. Skinny pale green stems covered in dusky oval-shaped leaves had already grown several inches high, and the lavender in front of her was still growing. A squawk of amazement hitched in her throat. Jax pushed both of the red pots away and took a few steps back. She hadn't known what to anticipate but certainly not that. She stared down at her dirt-splotched fingers, flipping her hands over. There were crescents of soil under her fingernails and smudged into the creases of her palms, but her hands looked like ordinary hands.

Jaxon anxiously looked around to make sure no one was watching. She realized belatedly there was a single camera in the top corner of the green-house, and she remembered the whole campus was always under surveillance. She prayed whoever might be watching would assume their eyes were playing tricks on them.

A pins-and-needles sensation persisted in her feet. She wondered if it had anything to do with her newfound ability to make things grow. She wondered about the lure of the gardens. Why was she able to do those things? Jax sucked in an anxious breath and reached for the last pot of soil. She dusted off her hands and cautiously grabbed the last envelope of seeds. The same thing happened with the thyme. Everything she touched grew, and the more things grew, the closer she felt a connection with the earth. What was she?

Jax shook her head at the question. It was enough for the day. She had barely been in the greenhouse for a half hour, and already she had three pots growing healthy herbs. She hid them beneath a shelf so Dr. Hollis, with his water experiments, wouldn't see them and ask questions. If anyone asked, she would tell them she hadn't lingered in the greenhouse; she had spent the evening in group fitness. Jaxon tore out of the greenhouse and jogged across the yard to the house. She crashed through the kitchen door, jogged into the hallway, and took the stairs down to the basement, scrubbing her hands on her jeans as she went.

"Jaxon!" Loren called out when she made it to the gym. Otto looked up from the weight bench and smiled.

"Hey," Jax said shyly.

"Get over here," Loren said. "We thought you weren't going to make it down this evening. Glad you finally made an appearance. Want to throw some punches with me?"

Jaxon spent the rest of the evening slap boxing with Loren, an event that once again drew a crowd and forced Jax to hold back her true strength. It was fun to get rough and physical, to play-fight with someone who wasn't really trying to hurt her. As she bounced around the room, boxing and avoiding getting hit, she found herself getting more relaxed with the basement regulars, but Jaxon couldn't keep her eyes off Otto.

"You're a fast learner. You're getting better already," he said after the match. "Let's get you hydrated. You're sweating like crazy."

Jaxon blushed when she realized he was right. "Oh, I'm sorry." He shook his head and grinned, waving away her concerns, but Jaxon stared down self-consciously. Her denim shirt was drenched, and her hair was all over her head, the wavy hair curling and frizzing in the humidity. She hadn't paid attention to any of that while she was working out with Loren, but she was starkly aware of it with him. Otto beckoned, and Jax nervously followed him up the stairs.

"Don't worry about how you look. You look amazing to me." The way he said the words made the hairs along the nape of her neck stand at attention. Jaxon smiled, flattered but skeptical.

"Really?" she asked.

They exited the basement and crossed the foyer to the dining hall. He smiled and handed her a water bottle from the buffet table, then he led her out to the side patio. They sat together with Jaxon fighting the butterflies that threatened to steal her breath. Otto looked introspective and stayed mute, gazing at the horizon. She studied him.

Otto pointed at the faint first sprinkling of stars. "You ever wonder what's up there?" Jaxon looked up and saw a crescent moon in the evening sky. She shrugged. What was to wonder? There was enough going on in her life down there. Otto gave a disparaging laugh and shook his head ruefully. "It's funny, but I used to think there were other life forms in the universe just waiting for humans to get their crap together so they could beam us up... I don't think they'll ever do it. We got a lot of hang-ups."

Jaxon shrugged again, staring at his handsome face. "I never really gave it much thought. When I was a kid, I was too busy trying to protect myself from malicious foster parents and messed-up living arrangements. That's the stuff you ponder when you don't have to worry about real life." She didn't mean to sound so harsh, but the memories were hard to shake. She was glad she would soon be out of the system. Jaxon heaved a gusty sigh and dropped her gaze. When she looked up, she caught Otto staring at her. "What?" she asked.

"What happened to your parents?"

"I don't know." She lifted her shoulders. "Maybe they got beamed up. Maybe they had all their crap together, and they didn't need me to muck up their travel arrangements. I don't know."

She smiled to take the sting out of her words. Otto reached across the back of the bench where they sat and pulled her closer. Jaxon stiffened, not used to comfort. He kissed the top of her head and pulled her down on his shoulder, resting his cheek against her hair. "I hope your future makes your past tremble, Jaxon Andersen," he whispered. "I hope you live such a beautiful life that it makes up for everything that came before."

The expression was such a delicate wish that Jaxon felt rare tears sting her eyes, and she quickly dashed them away. "That's sweet," she whispered. They sat in companionable silence for the rest of the hour allotted to extracurriculars. When it was time for students to come in at five thirty and get ready for dinner and bed, he released her and walked her to her room. His fingers, which were wrapped around hers, felt warm and natural. She knew there were other residents filing past, but she didn't pay them any mind. She didn't want whatever was happening between her and Otto to end.

"Well... thank you," Jaxon said nervously as she fondled the doorknob to her room. "Thank you for all you're doing to make my experience here wonderful. You're a nice guy."

"Not always. I like you," he confessed, grinning. "I'm sure that has something to do with it."

Jax giggled, suddenly looking at her feet. She inhaled deeply and gazed up into his eyes. "I like you, too."

"I think I might like you more than I like fires..." The eye contact intensified by several degrees. Jaxon felt dizzy under his spell. "See you at dinner. Will you sit with me?" She nodded. When he turned around and walked off down the hall to the boys' half of the house, he left her staring after him with her mouth slightly agape.

Jaxon opened the door and entered her room, her heart hammering. "Did he just say what I think he said?" she whispered to herself. She pushed away from the door to hurry to her closet to find something to wear to the dining hall. She was so wrapped up in romance that she had completely forgotten what had happened before, what had happened in the greenhouse. Her magic.

APRIL 16, 2016, SAN FRANCISCO, CALIFORNIA
9:25 PM

Anthony Hollis moved the cursor back to the start of the video clip. He played it again on double speed. In the clip, Jaxon entered the greenhouse. The supplies were on the table. The pots were empty. Before Jaxon exited the greenhouse, she hid the pots.

It was the director's suggestion to monitor the girl. After all, she was having unsupervised time alone in the garden. She could be out there growing God knew what. She could be sneaking out there to smoke cigarettes or hook up with boys or any clandestine thing that was against the group home's policy. Anthony didn't believe she would do anything amiss, but he had to follow the director's request and keep an eye on her, namely because if anything happened to Jaxon, Forever Welcome would be held liable.

It was Saturday night, and technically Anthony was off work. He had intended to take a quick glance at the surveillance video and get to bed. But something about the video from Wednesday—Jaxon's first and only day alone in the greenhouse since she had started gardening as her extracurricular—wasn't adding up.

He played the video again, slower, slower. He watched her plant the seeds. Anthony squinted his eyes to study the image closer. Then, his eyes widened as he caught a glimpse over Jaxon's shoulder of the plants that seemed to materialize out of nowhere. He shook his head in disbelief. "What the heck was that? What was she doing out there?" There was no way she should have had plants growing.

"I need to see this for myself," he mumbled.

Anthony put on his shoes and exited his apartment on the third floor. He went down the back staircase that led from his corner of the house to the backyard, and he loped across the green grass to the secret garden. He ran out to the greenhouse, determined to see with his own eyes what Jaxon had planted. The rapid growth on the video had to be a trick of the light. He knew Jax had requested herbs, noting that they were quick and easy to grow, but herbs didn't grow that fast.

Anthony powered on the lights and went directly to her hiding spot, having watched her on the video as she placed the pots beneath a shelf. When he pulled out the three small earthen pots, his heart skipped a beat. They were overflowing with fully grown plants, exactly as the video taken three days prior had shown, which was downright impossible. The pots should have been filled with rich, fertile potting soil, possibly a tiny sprout or two, but there was no imagining the leafy, fragrant lavender and spicy sweet marjoram. They were there.

What he had seen on the video had been real, not a trick of the light or sleight of hand. Anthony shook his head. "That can't be. That's not how it works. How on earth did she pull this off?" He struggled to get his cell phone out of his pocket. "Brady? Hello, dear friend. Listen, I need to send you a video, and I need you to tell me what you see when you look at it. Tell me I'm not losing my mind."

"What is it, Anthony? I'm in the middle of dinner. This better not be any of that Emoto nonsense."

"S-stranger than that, actually," Anthony stammered. "The girl I told you about, remember her? Jaxon? Well, I think... I think she's got even more special capabilities than... humanly possible? I-I'm not really sure how to explain. You'll just have to check the email, friend. As soon as possible, please!"

"Of course, of course, I will. As soon as I leave the restaurant, I'll check it. Now, get some sleep. It's rather late, and you sound like you need it."

Anthony Hollis hung up his phone with shaking hands and placed the potted plants back in their hiding place. He hurried back to his room to compile the message to send Brady. How could he explain it? How was he to put into words that the girl with the genius IQ could make plants sprout out of thin air? There had to be a reasonable explanation.

Anthony sat back on his bed and contemplated the facts. He couldn't run with the fanciful. He had to think logically. Jaxon must have secretly concocted some type of cell growth serum that resulted in the rapid maturation of plant cells. That had to be it. She was smart enough to do it, but even if that were the case, Anthony was equally stunned at the implications of such a scientific discovery. She was only sixteen. "She's a walking marvel," he said, a slow grin spilling across his bearded face. "She could probably get into any college in the country with something like this."

He laughed, his head full of ideas on how to get her further in life. He had never had a more brilliant student, and Anthony intended to use every resource at his disposal to ensure Jaxon didn't sleep on her gifts. He needed to call her into his office and have that chat again about her future. But first, he would email Brady with the evidence to make sure he wasn't just imagining things. Anthony knew his colleague thought he was a little loopy sometimes, but there would be no refuting what was on that video.

As he hurriedly composed the email, he wondered if maybe the news should be relayed in person rather than over the Internet. Anyone could gain access to an email if the recipient was unwary. Hell, Brady might even take a notion to forward it to someone. Anthony had to act with caution. He could trust Brady, but he would have to insist his friend keep the matter strictly confidential. "For your eyes only," Anthony read aloud as he typed. The last thing Anthony needed was some fertilizer company or research team trying to capitalize on Jaxon's hard work.

He didn't realize that—thanks to his method of communication—with or without Brady willfully sharing the details of the message, someone else was keeping a close watch on Jaxon Andersen, too. Someone with less than positive motivations.

APRIL 16, 2016, SAN FRANCISCO, CALIFORNIA

11:25 PM

Light tapping at her door woke Jaxon from a sound sleep, and she rolled over in bed to investigate the source of the noise. It was rare to be awakened in the night at Forever Welcome. She had a brief mental image of Otto and threw off her covers, reaching for a robe to see if it could be him, but it wasn't. Jax leaned out the door and peered up and down the hall. No one was there, but something was on the floor. Written in scarlet-red lipstick and in tiny letters was a hateful poem—if it could be called that. Jax planted her hands on her hips and smacked her lips as she read the tasteless drivel.

Jaxon Andersen is diseased

She sleeps with every guy she please

Although she thinks she's hot to trot

She's really, really not

The longer she stared at the words, the more Jaxon felt her blood boil. She knew who had written them. Only Lizzie would be trashy enough to mark up the hardwood floor with a vile shade of red lipstick. Jax swallowed a scream. "This has got to stop!"

She marched into her bathroom and dug out a terry cloth towel and bar of soap, the only cleaning supplies lying around. She couldn't let everyone get up in the morning and see what Lizzie had written. She wouldn't give the girl the pleasure of getting that much attention. Jax got down on her hands and knees and started to scrub the floor. Her arms burned with the exertion and the strain of holding her anger in check.

She scrubbed in swirly circles until the soap suds were pink from the lipstick. Jaxon went back in her room to wash the towel and then go over the floor again. She bit her lip to keep from crying. She still hadn't gotten Dr. Hollis involved because she wanted to fend for herself, but things were getting out of hand. Lizzie had vandalized school property. Who was to say someone wouldn't notice some residual marking and think Jaxon had done it? It was right outside her door.

Over and over, she replayed visions of getting back at Lizzie, each creative idea more gruesome than the last. She wanted to smear her face with lipstick. She wanted to tear out her hair. Jax trembled with rage. When she was finished cleaning the floor as well as possible, she tiptoed down the stairs.

Jaxon crept to the basement to let off steam. There was no way she could go back to sleep after what had happened. The lights were off, and the exercise equipment was powered down. The basement was an eerie place after hours, without the other residents to add life and laughter. She hit the lights, and she ambled to her favorite part of the gym. She picked up the boxing gloves hanging from a hook next to the punching bag.

Jax slid them onto her fists. She could finally unleash her full potential. She didn't notice the security camera slowly swivel to watch her as she started to throw jabs. At first, she gave the heavy bag a few light taps, warming up, blow after blow barely shifting it. As she considered all the things Lizzie had done to her since her arrival, Jaxon begin to hit harder.

"Think you can mess with me and get away with it? Unh!" Jaxon's punch powered into the faded leather with a loud thwack. She hit it again. "Think just because you're bigger than me, you're better than me?" The punishing attacks caused the punching bag to jostle on its chain, sway, and shiver with the hits. She punched again. "You don't know who you're playing with, girl!" Jaxon spun around and kicked with all her might. Her shin connected with the bag, and the cement-weighted leather cylinder flew off its hook.

"Dang it!" Jax reached for it before it hit the floor, but it slipped out of her grasp.

The punching bag smashed into the wall with an explosive thump. Jaxon jumped, looking up at the basement ceiling and listening for approaching footsteps. She ran to the punching bag and hefted it up in her hands. She handled the hundred-pound bundle as easily as a light backpack. She slung it on her shoulder and was about to take it back over to the hook, hoping no one upstairs had heard the noise.

That was when she saw him. Otto stood at the foot of the stairs watching her with eyes round as saucers. He had a white-knuckle grip on the handrail. His pulse was visibly heightened, a throbbing vein at his temple. He looked as if it was taking everything in him not to bolt back up the stairs and get away from her.

"I was—I was—" Jaxon struggled to find an explanation for what Otto had seen. The bag rolled down from her shoulder and hit the floor with a loud thud.

Otto cautiously stepped down onto the black foam. He eased closer but not close enough for her to reach for him. He looked as if he didn't trust her not to put a whipping on him as she had the punching bag. Otto warily asked, "How did you do that?"

"I, um..." Jaxon's face crumpled. Why had he snuck up on her? She didn't know what to say, and she liked him too much to think of him not liking her back, but there was no way anyone could witness what he had and see her as anything but a freak. She threw her slender brown hand to her forehead and blew out an exasperated breath. "Look, don't tell anybody about what you think you just saw, all right?" She toughened up. The least he could do was give her the dignity of keeping her secret, even if he cut her out of his romantic picture.

"Do it again," he ordered.

Jaxon looked up.

"Hit it again. I want to see what you can really do."

"Why?" she said forcefully. "So you can look at me like I'm some kind of circus attraction? Get real, Otto. Just forget you ever saw anything." She hardened her voice and balled her fists. If she wanted to, she could really hurt him. She would never do that, but maybe if she made Otto believe she was a threat, he would keep his mouth shut.

At the sight of her tiny, trembling frame and her eyes glistening with tears, Otto walked closer, unafraid. "Stop it. I'm not gonna tell anyone, Jaxon." He reached out for her hand, pulled off the boxing glove, and examined her knuckles. They weren't even bruised. He looked at the punching bag and back at the slight girl who barely topped out at his chin height. "Show me again what you can do," he coaxed. He wanted to know everything about her. She had him completely captivated.

Jaxon warily accepted the glove and put it back on. "If I show you this, you have to swear to me that this stays in this basement. You can't breathe a word about this to anyone. Do you understand me? People can't know that I'm a..."

"What?" he asked softly.

"A freak."

He chucked up her chin and looked in her sparkling, ice chip–blue eyes. "Babe, from what I just saw, you're not a freak... you're the eighth world wonder."

He tapped her fists and pointed her to the punching bag. She picked it up and mounted it back on its chain. Jaxon swallowed her fear. He was watching. She wanted to make a good impression. She took a deep breath and squared her shoulders. As her shoulder blades widened and she put up her fists, time slowed to a crawl for the girl who wasn't anything like other girls. The white T-shirt and pixie-print lavender pajama pants swooshed forward in an elegant blur as her long, rangy arms shot out one after the other, fists connecting with the black leather with biting force.

She grunted softly with each blow. Her feet came off the floor, and she seemed to dance. She floated on air. She kicked with her shins and hit with her elbows. She grabbed the swaying bag and went harder with a punch, punch, spin-kick, four punches in rapid succession, flip, spin-kick, jab—moves that had Otto's eyebrows lifting higher and higher, his mouth open in amazement.

She spun away from the punching bag and flipped up into the air, then she barreled down to the floor to land in a roll and come back up on her feet before him, not even winded by the effort. He reached for her and pulled her against his chest. "Whatever you are," he said in awe, "you're something special."

Jaxon smiled and pushed out of his embrace. "And you're breaking the rules, RA. You know we're not supposed to be down here alone after dark. Come on. Let's get out of here." She strolled to the stairs, and he trailed her. Jax glanced over her shoulder and said, "My reason for being here is taken care of now, anyway. Stupid Lizzie Baptiste wrote on the floor in front of my room with a red lipstick pencil, and I had to clean it up. Gah! She has no idea how close she comes to being ripped in half sometimes."

"To think I wanted to make you a part of the fitness club to give you some pointers on how to defend yourself." Otto chuckled ruefully. "You really could give her the business, and she'd never know what hit her. But don't worry about Lizzie anymore. For her sake, I'll write her up and get points docked so she can learn to leave you alone. How long have you been able to do that kind of stuff?" He dropped his voice as they entered the hallway on the ground floor.

Jaxon shrugged. "All my life, really," she whispered. "I've always been stronger, smarter, faster than others." She bit her bottom lip uncertainly. "That's not all, either."

His eyes were ashy embers in the dark. "What else can you do?"

"I could show you, but Otto, you really can't tell anyone. You can't even hint at it. Do you know what they do to people like me? They lock us up in science labs and run experiments on us. Or worse, they don't believe we're telling the truth and throw us into loony bins." She paused at the threshold of the kitchen's back door, preparing to take him to the backyard. "I just want to live a normal life."

Otto opened the door and stepped out. He thought Jaxon was anything but normal, but he replied, "Your secret is safe with me. You can trust me, Jaxon."

The moon was a white sliver in the black sky above. It was a starry night, and so far from the lights of the city, Jaxon could see it clearly for the first time. She hadn't been outside after dark since she had arrived at the facility. "Look at that," she breathed in amazement, looking up. She could almost imagine those other life forms that Otto had been talking about earlier really existed. She pointed as a brilliant flash of light shot across the sky.

"A shooting star," Otto said. "Make a wish." Jaxon closed her eyes and tried to come up with something to wish for, but she wasn't made like that. She didn't believe in making wishes. She worked for what she wanted and hoped for the best. "What did you wish?" he asked.

"If I tell you, it won't come true," she replied.

"Oh, is that how it works?" He chuckled.

"That's what I always heard." Jax walked across the patio and stepped down from the porch to the green lawn. "Come see." She touched the slightly damp grass. At the spot she touched, a flash of hazy fluorescence illuminated the darkness. Jax tried a twist to the growth magic she had used in the greenhouse, knowing instinctively it would work. She closed her eyes and envisioned a peace lily.

She felt the tingles in her fingers and under her toes. She felt the earth begin to respond. There was a shifting in the soil beneath the grass, and suddenly the blades parted. A single dark leaf pushed up from the ground, followed by another. A thick stem shot up, capped by a white lily. Jaxon covered her mouth in amazement. "See?" When she looked at Otto, he was staring at the flower as if he couldn't believe what he was seeing. He kneeled to the ground and touched it to see if it was real. The faint scent wafted to his nose. Jaxon gently pulled up the plant and slung it under the porch. "So, yeah, it gets weirder. Now you know why I don't want anyone else to find out."

Chapter 10

APRIL 22, 2016, SAN FRANCISCO,
CALIFORNIA

11:00 AM

Although Otto was able to keep Jaxon's secret, Anthony Hollis was unwittingly exposing her at every turn. He fired off emails to Brady and made phone calls in the night to verify his findings. He had sent a sample of the plants she had grown to a friend who was a botanist to determine the authenticity. Dr. Hollis didn't know what to do with the results. He could only compile the evidence and ponder what it meant for Forever Welcome that she was a resident.

He had to think of her best interests. He didn't want to say or do anything that would alert the media. She didn't need the scrutiny. Instead, he had to focus on how she could utilize her gifts to get into a degree program at a prestigious university. "Imagine what her product could do, Brady. She could virtually cure world hunger." He spoke into the phone, peering out the window of his office, although he couldn't see the greenhouse from his vantage point. It had been two weeks since he had seen the initial video surveillance clip, and Anthony was antsy for the girl to get back out there and do some more botany experimenting.

Jaxon was getting along much better with the others at the group home, and he noticed she had sparked a romance with Otto Heike, the resident assistant. He worried her social life might supersede her academics. She was still doing well in her courses, and she had even submitted a list of colleges to which she wanted to apply. Anthony had the paperwork ready for her to take her SAT. But all that seemed trivial in comparison to what she could truly do. He needed Jaxon to stay focused on the science.

Anthony scribbled a reminder to meet with her after class and stuck the note to his computer. Brady was saying, "It's hard to wrap my mind around, I have to admit. You have a penchant for believing in the craziest things. I wonder, could this be your imagination getting away from you? Have you even talked to the girl about it?"

"No, but I'm going to this evening. But you've seen the videos, man. Soon we'll have the analysis of the first plants she grew."

"Just don't go get your hopes too high," Brady warned.

A knock at the door got Anthony's attention. "I'll have to call you back, friend." A resident ambled into his office and dropped down into the dining chair in front of Anthony's desk as the psychiatrist gazed at him expectantly. "What can I do for you, Otto?"

"I just came to report that Jaxon is still having problems with another one of the girls, although she didn't want me to tell you because she didn't want to seem like she was ratting someone out."

"Ha! She told me something along those lines when I asked her about it, too." Anthony smiled.

Otto said, "I've taken the time to get to know Jax, sir. She keeps to herself, doesn't bother anyone. Truth be told, she's a little shy. The problem is Lizzie. Last night, she used a lipstick to write an ugly message outside Jaxon's door. She's also been terrorizing her in the restrooms and anywhere else she can get her alone. I did a formal RA complaint write-up. I also gave Jaxon the RAs' phone numbers so she could call or text the next time she had an issue with her since she isn't comfortable talking directly to you about it."

He handed the doctor the paperwork. Anthony perused the form and nodded, sticking it in the top drawer of his desk. "Of course. I'll take care of this. Eh, while I have you here, Otto, I noticed you and Jaxon have been getting close. I wonder, has she mentioned anything to you about a plant experiment or a science project? Anything like that?"

The resident assistant's eyelids flickered at the word plant, but he tried to remain expressionless. Anthony caught the brief response, however. "No, not at all," Otto lied.

"Are you sure about that? I'm trying to compile a list of undergraduate major programs for her, and I need to know her interests. I will ask her myself, but I thought you might know."

"Um, she likes flowers and stuff."

"Has she shown you her gardening skills, by chance?"

Otto clammed up, his lips a tight line. He shrugged his shoulders and shook his head. Anthony considered it confirmation that Jaxon was, in fact, working on a top-secret science experiment. He thanked Otto for stopping by and sent him back to class. When the boy left, Anthony sat back, satisfied with the answers he had gotten. He sent an email to the teachers to have Jaxon stop by his office after class. They had a lot to discuss.

APRIL 22, 2016, SAN FRANCISCO, CALIFORNIA
5:35 PM

She sat next to Otto on top of the picnic table under the ginkgo tree, watching the other residents engaged in a lively game of volleyball. Because it was Friday, the normal extracurricular activities were exchanged for an evening of group play, but the couple sat off to the side to talk about why Dr. Hollis had called her into his office. Jaxon toyed with the frayed hem of her jean skirt as she spoke, her mind dizzy with worries. "He asked me about the greenhouse. I don't know what to tell him. He's convinced I'm hiding some secret chemical formulation that makes plants grow faster," she said. "I wish he would just leave it alone."

"I told you at lunch, he was probing me when I dropped in with Lizzie's write-up. Why don't you tell him what he wants to hear? Hell, put some water in a bottle and make him believe it's the formula. That'll keep him from finding out how you really do it." Otto chuckled, knowing his suggestion was out of the question but wanting to make her laugh.

She giggled briefly, looking away with haunted eyes again after a moment. The psychiatrist had apparently wanted to discuss her future plans. Otto knew from past experience that wasn't the way Dr. Hollis usually handled things, but then again, Jaxon wasn't the usual student.

"If I knew why I am the way I am, it would make me feel a lot more comfortable. It's weird, you know? I'm a mystery even to myself. Anyway, thanks for handling the situation with Lizzie for me. I heard she got, like, thirty points taken away. Hopefully, she got the message."

He put his hand over hers and squeezed her fingers. "Jax, what are you going to do if anyone does find out?"

She shrugged. "Prepare myself for the worst," she said. She shivered, a sense of premonition hanging over her. Later, she lay awake thinking about Otto's question. The truth was, she had hid her special qualities all her life because she knew that people wouldn't accept someone so strange, so different. They destroyed things they didn't understand. She worried that nothing positive could happen from others knowing, and she wondered for the first time if—instead of providing her with the tools necessary to get out into the real world once she matriculated out of the foster care system—Forever Welcome would turn out to be her undoing.

APRIL 25, 2016, UTAH DATA CENTER
9:00 AM

Gerard Terrace, the intelligence analyst, studied the information compiled on case number 6458181b. "She's young," he said to General Meade. "Younger than all the other participants. I don't know if she'll work for the program."

"Don't bother yourself with that, Terrace. Her youth is going to work in our favor. Has the information been verified?"

"We're still in beta phase, verifying. Once she's cleared, I'll have the information compiled in a more cohesive report and released to you. Then, Dr. Yamazaki can start phase delta of preliminary genetic testing." Gerard gestured to the woman sitting across from his desk. She inclined her head demurely. She hadn't said a word the whole meeting.

"Actually," said General Meade, turning away from Gerard's visual display board where he had been perusing the case file on the teenage subject, "we have to tread lightly here because she's a minor. We're not going to be able to use the same ruse we used on the others to get her out to Starke. Fortunately, there aren't any parents to badger for approval, but she's a ward of the state."

"What do you propose?" asked Gerard.

"I've already got something in the works," General Meade said, but he had no intention of ever revealing the full plan to Gerard. The intelligence analyst didn't have the security clearance to know everything that was going on. He was just a pawn in an elaborate network of pieces powering forward to an end goal none of them understood—except Meade.

A smile slid across the general's clean-shaven face. His sparse eyebrows joined over his deep-set eyes, and he heaved a relaxed sigh as he faced Gerard. "Just get me everything you know about the girl, from past to current."

"That, as it turns out, will be the easiest part. The group home utilizes a security surveillance center that uploads to a cloud. In this case, we damn near have full access to her life. We know what time she wakes up, what she eats for dinner. We know her foes and friends, her love interests, her favorite teachers. Hell, we know her diary password. IQ off the charts. History of physical altercations, abnormal strength for size. I have to say, General Meade, she fits the profile."

"That she does, my friend. Now, I have to get back to the compound. Gerard, keep me posted. Dr. Yamazaki?"

The general and the doctor who had come with him strolled out of the intelligence data collecting building. Meade climbed into his black sedan with a weary grunt. He was wearing civilian clothes and looked like somebody's grandfather. Hector Meade chuckled to himself. He didn't have a wife, much less kids or grandkids. He had dedicated his entire life to the pursuit of one thing—keeping his country protected from outside threats.

He had worked closely with nearly every secret department within the government. The titles changed, and the directors changed, but their purposes never changed, and right then, General Meade was in charge of one of the most secretive projects of his career. America faced a new threat. One without borders. One with technology far more advanced than anything on earth.

For over thirty years, he had monitored the sightings, the encounters, the vanishings. Although the official report was that extraterrestrials were the stuff of science fiction, Meade knew "they" were out there. And the particular intergalactic travelers he was currently concerned with presented the greatest danger. He knew what they wanted; they were abducting people with the Atlantis gene. He just didn't know exactly what they were doing with them once they got them. It was his job to get to the Atlantis descendants first and study them so he could know his enemy.

Meade had explained all that to the inquisitive geneticist on their second trip to the database. He had done so because she was one of few involved who had the security clearance to hear the full plan. Technically, they were equals. "So, you see, Dr. Yamazaki, time is of the essence," he murmured. "That's why you're so integral to this process. Without you, we wouldn't be able to separate the chaff from the wheat without losing precious decades trying to sift through the mess for genetic matches. Our enemy is on the same mission."

"We can't let *them* get to the people on the list before we do," Akiko whispered. It was a lot to take in. Everything she had learned in her few days with General Meade left her more confused than satisfied with answers. She knew what the general was implying—that little green men were flitting about the earth gathering up a specific demographic—but could it be real? Akiko lowered her head and kept her thoughts to herself as the black sedan drove back to the airport where they would fly to New Mexico, home of Starke Genetics.

"Why do you think they want the Atlantis descendants?" she asked.

"To use them against us, of course." General Meade responded like a wise elder speaking to a very young child. "Possibly to build up an army or something like sleeper cells. Why else would they be implanting their DNA into our human genome? They need a race of hybrids who can survive our atmosphere, our earth. I'm almost certain they're doing this because they're planning some type of large-scale attack."

"But there are so few of them," Akiko said. "In our search, we've only found six real matches out of tens of thousands of potentials. That's not enough for an army or large-scale attack. What if there's another reason? Let's say their species has become depleted, too inbred to produce viable offspring, and they need new genetic material to offset the problems caused by consanguinity—descending from the same ancestor."

Meade waved away her explanation. "Either way, we're humans. We're better off protecting the human half of those creatures. We can't let them get into alien hands."

She swallowed and nodded in agreement. "What have we been doing with them once we find them?" That was the real question, the reason she had made it a point to schedule a conference with General Meade and tell him she needed to know what was going on in order to do her job. He chuckled.

"Don't worry your pretty little head about that, Dr. Yamazaki. They're safe, alive, and well."

She thought about the horrid room with the freezer drawers, the bodies of the patients with the Atlantis gene suspended in a comatose state and kept on ice for... for whatever eventuality General Meade dreamed up. Akiko gritted her teeth and set her jaw. Yes, they were alive, but well was subjective. And Meade and his intelligence analyst were plotting to do the same thing to a child.

Akiko struggled to hide her trembling. How Meade could be so unethical and unfeeling was completely beyond her. He had to be crazy to think she would subject an innocent child to the testing, poking, and prodding she had been a fool to allow herself to take part in from the very beginning. She wouldn't continue the madness. There had to be some way to get word to the teenager. The geneticist contemplated sending a message, but every electronic, digital, or telephone communication would be intercepted by Gerard and his watchful eyes and ears. She couldn't have anything traced to her.

Akiko was convinced she wouldn't be able to lie on the test results, either. Thanks to the intelligence analyst, Meade would have more than enough evidence to the contrary, even if she said the subject wasn't a match. The girl fit the profile. She had the characteristic hyperintelligence. She had the unique botany abilities that Akiko hadn't seen in any other patients. She didn't know if the girl was just as strong or fast as the other participants, but she had a history of strength disproportionate to her size. Akiko had no idea if the girl could read minds or use mental powers to move objects around, but the patient had all the other signs of an Atlantis gene carrier.

They traveled the rest of the trip in silence. Across the seat from Akiko, General Meade was too wrapped up in his own thoughts to pay her any mind. He needed to figure out how to get the teenager under his care, and he had to do it in a way that wouldn't get any dirt on his hands.

The initial six subjects were over twenty-five and had health challenges from poor eating habits, smoking, and drinking. None of them were suitable for anything more than harvesting stem cells and studying their genomes. With a young, healthy, viable subject like the teenager, the possibilities were endless for what could transpire. Meade envisioned a prototype special agent with the Atlantis gene, one capable of feats no human counterpart could match. With training, education, and the remolding of her psyche, this Jaxon Ares Andersen could be the one.

He rubbed his hands together restlessly. Soon, very soon, she would be his.

Chapter 11

APRIL 25, 2016, SAN FRANCISCO,
CALIFORNIA

11:00 AM

There was a tap on Anthony's doorframe, and he glanced up to see the director of the group home. "Uh, I'll call you back, Brady." He hastily hung up the phone and smiled at Mr. Vance. "What can I do for you, sir?" He had been trying to find out if Brady would come down for the Forever Welcome group home Annual Friends and Family Day. Once a year, the residents were allowed to invite outsiders to come see their home. It was the opportune time to get Brady to meet Jaxon, but that conversation would have to wait. The director of the facility appeared to be in a hurry.

The gray-haired man in the sable three-piece suit ambled into the office with a folder in hand. "Not here to chat. I'm already late. Just stopped by to drop off a file for an incoming student."

"Ah! Another newbie." Anthony brightened. He accepted the thin file. "Male or female?"

"Sixteen-year-old girl. Make sure you get her placed and settled. I won't be here for the intake. Do we have to move around anybody to make room? I can't remember the last demographic printout."

"Not at all, sir. The last resident, Jaxon Andersen, has a free bed in her room. Oh, sir, I wanted to talk to you about Jaxon when you get a moment." It occurred to Anthony he could ask the facility director how best to promote Jaxon's excellence without leaving her prey to exploitation.

"It will have to wait until I get back, Hollis. I've got a plane to catch and a vacation to enjoy. Good riddance to babysitting overgrown teenagers." Mr. Vance chuckled.

"Forgot you were off the rest of the week."

"You'd think with all those sticky notes, you'd be more on top of things. Please tell me you have everything together for the open house next month."

"Got it covered," said Anthony. He had only a few preparations left, but he'd have things in place once classes were over for the semester. Anthony had already met with the rest of the staff to get the grounds ready, and he had a shipment of party supplies on the way. Invitations were being sent by the residents.

Mr. Albert Vance breezed through the arch but tossed a word of advice over his shoulder. "Oh, and Anthony, do something about this place, would you? You realize you don't have a door to hide this mess behind."

"Will do, sir." With a sigh, Anthony flipped open the file folder for the new resident and perused the contents. Loose papers slipped from his desk, but he didn't notice. There was always something slipping, sliding, or falling in his cluttered office. The new resident was Ginger Edwards. Interestingly enough, there was little information on her background. The file contained only her name, date of birth, blood type and health information, emergency contact numbers, and transcript with her grades.

He frowned at the lack of accompanying paperwork. "Maybe her caseworker will bring it over when he or she gets here." He shrugged his shoulders and set the folder aside. Anthony wrote a quick note and ran upstairs to Jaxon's room. He hoped she wouldn't mind. In fact, he knew she probably wouldn't. The girl outside playing with other residents was a far cry from the girl who had first arrived at the group home. Anthony said with pleasure as he went back to his office, "Well, it can't be a bad thing that she's finally coming into herself."

Chapter 12

APRIL 25, 2016, SAN FRANCISCO,
CALIFORNIA
3:30 PM

She was getting a roommate. Jaxon
had received the message when she
came in from extracurriculars, spent
down in the basement with Otto and his
friends. She stared at the note from Dr.
Hollis and chewed on a fingernail, trying
to decide whether the news was a good
thing or a bad thing. She had been at
Forever Welcome group home for over
two months, and that was probably the
longest stretch of time in her life that

she'd had a room to herself. She glanced over at the half of the room that still looked untouched and pristine. Jaxon had hardly taken up all the space.

The evening sunlight pierced through the blinds of the bay window, slanted across the black duvet, and lit the green throw pillows on the narrow twin bed. The writing desk that wasn't in use had a thin layer of dust coating the surface, while Jaxon's desk was neatly organized with a stack of workbooks, her smartphone perched on a corner and charging. There were still empty drawers in the dresser bureau and still room in the closet for someone else's belongings. She had known from the very beginning—Dr. Hollis had warned her—she would eventually have to share that space with someone else. She just wondered what sort of person she would be rooming with and whether she could get used to having her sanctuary invaded by someone else again.

In the time she had been at the group home, Jaxon found that the experience had lived up to her expectations. She had been prepared for the bullying because Jaxon had dealt with being picked on and harassed nearly all her life. She wasn't surprised by the structured environment and rigorous class schedules, either. Considering the group home was an award-winning facility, of course they would push their residents to excel. While she had been scared out of her wits the day Dr. Hollis told her he was putting her in advanced placement classes, she was doing well. Her final GPA reflected high marks across the board. But for all the encounters she had expected, Jax had also had some unexpected events along the way.

She had met and become close friends with some remarkable people. She respected and admired Dr. Hollis, despite his meddling. He had made it clear that he wanted only what was best for her. The psychiatrist was dreaming of university admissions and doctorates in her future. He was trying to prepare her for a world outside of foster care, and she appreciated his doggish tenacity, even if it meant she had to evade questions about the so-called top-secret plant formula he thought she had created.

Jaxon had a love interest, a thoughtful, intriguing guy who knew all her hidden capabilities and didn't look at her as if she was some kind of freak. It was strange and lovely that she could count on Otto to listen to her problems, to come to her aid when needed, and to make her feel included. Even more impressive, his acceptance of her led to other residents at the group home taking her into the flock and making Jaxon feel a part. Even Lizzie had scaled back her verbal jabs. Getting points docked and being scrutinized more closely after Otto wrote her up had forced the bully to leave Jaxon alone.

The most life-changing things that had happened, however, were deeply intimate and personal and had little to do with the residence itself. She was changing. She was growing into someone who didn't immediately lean toward distrust and defensiveness. Jax was still a fighter, but she didn't have to fight anymore. No longer focused on trying to stay one step ahead of her enemies, she was starting to focus more on herself, and the self-discoveries were only leading to more questions.

Jax dropped the note on the dresser bureau and stepped into her bathroom to shower and get dressed for dinner. Otto would be waiting.

She was different from other people. Otto knew that, but what would others think of her if they knew? Jaxon had always been vaguely aware she was abnormally strong. She had chalked it up to adrenaline rushes fueled by anger. Yet even when other people were angry, they couldn't do the things she could. And she had also added the trick with plants to her growing list of capabilities. Not for the first time, Jaxon wondered about her past. Who the heck was she? What was she?

She wondered how much longer she could keep what was happening to her a secret, especially with someone else in her personal space. Jax sighed and shook her head at her reflection. The more people who knew about her, the more danger she was in. She would have to tread carefully.

On Monday evening a week later, at the start of the new month, Ginger Edwards finally made her appearance. Jaxon almost missed her arrival, wrapped up as she was with preparations for final exams. The spring semester was coming to a close. She had reports and assignments due.

"Oh!" Jaxon had exclaimed, surprised. She had burst through the door in a rush to change into gym shorts and a T-shirt, determined not to make it to the basement in her day clothes. She had completely forgotten the girl was even coming until she walked into the room after classes and saw Ginger sitting on the bed. "I'm sorry. I didn't realize you were here already."

"Hi!" Ginger responded brightly. "Ginger Edwards. I'm your new roommate, but nobody told me your name, but that doesn't matter because now we have plenty of time to get to know each other. I'm so happy to meet you. I was wondering what you'd be like on the whole ride over here and hoping you'd be like the sister I've always wanted. I've always felt like an only child." She was bubbly and vivacious.

Ginger had translucent pale skin splashed with a smattering of brown freckles, eyes bluer than dawn, and coppery-red hair. She hopped up from the bed and rushed over to pull Jaxon into a tight hug.

Jax was taken aback, uncomfortable with the overly friendly girl's awkward embrace. Jaxon chuckled nervously to hide her uneasiness. "Um, nice to meet you, too."

Ginger grabbed her hand and pulled Jaxon over to her bed, plopping down with a cheerful smile and staring into Jaxon's face. "Tell me everything about you. I've been trying to picture you ever since I heard I'd have a roommate my age here. At first, I worried you'd be all, like, all dark and Goth or something. This place is for juvenile delinquents, after all. But you look so normal!"

Jax scooted away from her and laughed, a little overwhelmed. "I'm Jaxon," she murmured. "Boy, you're really excited to be here, aren't you?"

"Oh, yes. I'm a foster kid. I've been in a bunch of different group homes. I much prefer them to living with people who really don't want you but want a check for taking care of you, you know? I hate living with strange families."

Jaxon nodded, surprised to find out they had foster care in common. Many of the other residents were like Otto and came from regular homes, sent to Forever Welcome for minor criminal behavior. "Yeah, I know what you mean," Jax said, warming to her a little. Her vivaciousness would take some getting used to, but it was kind of cool to be rooming with another foster kid. Maybe the experience wouldn't be so bad after all. "So, uh, why are you here?" Jaxon asked.

Ginger's cornflower-blue eyes widened enigmatically. "This, that, or the other. Nothing too serious. I'm not dangerous or anything. I just don't fit in with regular society."

"Something else we have in common." Jaxon giggled. "Well, have you had your testing and placement with Dr. Hollis yet? How long have you been here?"

"Since this morning. I'm all placed. I can't wait to see what passes for school around here." Ginger chuckled and shook out a cigarette from a box in her purse. She put it to her lips and continued talking. "I hate school. I'm glad there's only a month left of class, but I'm amped to see what the extracurricular shit is about. Who's who around here? Are you going to show me around and help me get to know everybody?"

Jaxon eyed the cigarette nervously. "You can't smoke in here," she said.

Ginger rolled her eyes and pulled a pillowcase off her pillow, hurrying across the room and stuffing it in the crack at the base of the door. She came back and opened the windows, sitting on the window ledge as she lit up. "Relax, I'm not going to get you into any trouble. You want one?"

"I don't smoke," said Jax, growing even more wary. She wasn't interested in picking up any bad habits, either. Jax had a good track record at Forever Welcome. This new girl, for all her innocent appearance and gregarious personality, looked as if she was going to be a rule-breaker. "Uh, I'll let you get settled in. I was on my way down to the basement for gym."

Ginger took a long drag on the cigarette and snuffed it out on the windowsill, leaving a circular burn mark. Jaxon bit her tongue and backed into the bathroom to get dressed for gym. On the other side of the door, Ginger called out, "Cool beans! I'll come with."

"No, I'm sure you have unpacking to do," Jaxon replied.

"I told you, I've been here since morning, silly. I was sitting around here waiting for you. That Dr. Hollis guy said you'd be able to show me around."

Jaxon sighed. She wished Dr. Hollis had mentioned she would be playing tour guide. "Well, you might want to change out of the jeans and T-shirt and put on some active wear." Jax opened the bathroom door, dressed in nylon shorts and a tank top. She crossed the room to the closet and dug out her sneakers. "I'll wait for you." Fanning her face, Jaxon coughed. She hated the smell of cigarettes. She idly wondered if she should go ahead and report Ginger before she made smoking in the dorm room a regular activity. "But hurry up," Jax said gruffly. "Everyone else is probably already in the gym."

Ginger didn't seem to notice her gruff tone or reluctance to have her tag along. The new girl rushed into the bathroom with a handful of clothes she had dug out of her drawer. Jaxon bit her lips as she noticed the drawer was left half-open with more clothes falling out onto the floor. "Okay," she muttered under her breath. "This isn't going to work."

Jaxon decided to give her a week, reserving judgment and preferring to give Ginger time to get into the swing of things at Forever Welcome. She suffered through evenings of choking on Ginger's smoke, dealing with her new roommate's clutter, and having her ears talked off. The only person she told of the mismatched rooming situation was Otto.

They were having lunch outside on the patio when she complained, yet again, of Ginger's contradictory personality. "On the one hand," Jaxon said, spearing a forkful of food, "she's this bubbly personality who is easy to get along with. I find myself telling her all sorts of things about my past, because she's really easy to talk to. But she has this darker side, and I don't exactly trust her. When Lizzie tried to give her a hard time like she did me when I first got here, Ginger broke into her room. She told me she rubbed all Lizzie's T-shirts in poison ivy. Like, how sick and twisted is that?"

Otto hid a smile. "Serves Lizzie right. I'd talk to Ginger, if I were you. Try to make friends with her. Tell her what's cool here and what's not so she doesn't find herself in serious trouble with the director. The smoking in the room thing is serious. They'll do more than dock points for that. Everything else, though, just sounds like pranks and kid stuff.

Even the dirty room part. My roommate is a total slob, but as long as his crap doesn't end up on my side of the room, I deal with it."

The door to the dining hall opened, and Jaxon wasn't the least bit surprised to see Ginger standing there with a tray. "Speak of the devil," Jax muttered under her breath. Ever since the girl had gotten to the group home, Ginger seemed to make it a point to cling to Jaxon. Jax could barely go to the restroom without the girl following. She had been spared all week in the dining hall, but Jax had known all along that Ginger wouldn't respect her alone time with Otto forever.

Otto grinned and greeted the newest arrival. Ginger ducked her head apologetically. "Hate to bother you with your boyfriend, Jax."

"No, it's no problem. There's room at our table," Otto said with a friendly smile.

Ginger quickly crossed and put her tray down on the picnic table. "I don't really know anybody else inside. I hate eating alone. How's your day going, Jaxon? Anything exciting happen?"

Jax struggled not to roll her eyes. "The same ole same ole, but you've been there every step of the way. I hardly think you've missed anything."

Ginger burst out laughing. "You're so funny! Oh, I almost forgot. Dr. Hollis told me you do gardening in the greenhouse sometimes. I've always loved gardening. He said you'd be able to take me. Want to go today?"

Jaxon shrugged, frowning. She wasn't comfortable taking the strange new girl to her hideaway. With Dr. Hollis monitoring her actions in the greenhouse, Jaxon hadn't been back since mid-April and her first foray there. The last thing she needed was to take Ginger and have something weird happen with the plants while the girl was with her. "I thought you liked hanging out in the gym with us." Otto tried to rescue her. Jaxon shot him an appreciative smile.

Ginger shook her head. "To be honest, I'm not very athletic. I was just hanging out with you guys because Jaxon hangs out with you guys, but I'm really more salt of the earth than sweat of the brow, you know?"

Jaxon and Otto again shared a look. It sounded as if Dr. Hollis had found a new recruit in spying on Jaxon. Jax sighed. "We can go, but I'll just watch you. I'm, uh, allergic... to some of the plants in there. That's why I stopped going."

Ginger grinned. "Oh, wow! That's gotta suck. Gardening can be so peaceful. Is it a pollen allergy or something?"

"Not exactly." Jaxon slid Otto a sideways glance.

Otto replied, "She, um, broke out in hives? Right? Last time you were in there, Jaxon?"

"Exactly. And I don't know which plant is the culprit, so I just keep away from all the plants. I'll take you this one time, though, just to show you where everything is."

After classes were over, Jaxon fired off a text message to Otto saying "Wish me luck" and headed out to the greenhouse with Ginger. Ginger followed her across the backyard where a makeshift stage was being erected by the groundskeeper in front of the stone wall that led to the secret garden. The deck would eventually be surrounded by vibrant, colorful flower arrangements. The entire backyard area would be transformed in preparation for the event in two more weeks on May 20. According to Otto, there would be an awards ceremony, door prizes, and games. Jax was curious about how the Annual Friends and Family Day would play out. She knew Otto's parents were coming. The grounds would be swarming with people. She was already making plans to keep to herself.

Once within the rust-red framework of the greenhouse, Jaxon watched with waning interest as the new girl played in the dirt. Ginger coaxed and prodded Jaxon to join her, but Jax stayed back. She kept her hands in her pockets and listened to Ginger prattle on about nothing in particular. Ginger, she was discovering, had a knack for seeming to reveal a lot about herself while saying nothing at all. Ginger would hint at a history of delinquency but not exactly mention her past crimes. Jax knew Ginger was a foster kid, but while Ginger chatted endlessly about foster homes and group homes, the statements were pretty general.

"How long do you have in here?" Jaxon asked, curious to know more about the enigmatic girl.

"I don't keep up with all that stuff. I just go when and where they tell me to go. What about you?"

"A year and ten months left. So, why'd you say you were sent here, again?" Jaxon was perched against a lower shelf, out of Ginger's way. She watched the redhead fill a planter with potting soil and seeds, some from Jaxon's personal stash that hadn't been used since the first day in the greenhouse when her plants had grown impossibly fast. Jax was sweating and uncomfortable. It was muggy. Summer in San Francisco was much more intense than spring. She swiped perspiration from her brow, wishing Ginger would finish.

Ginger shrugged and replied evasively, "I'd rather not talk about that. That's in the past. I'm trying to turn over a new leaf. Ha! Pun intended!" She playfully threw a handful of seed at Jaxon.

Jaxon dashed out of the way before the seeds could touch her skin. "Hey!" she yelped. She could already feel the pins and needles in her toes and the tingles in her fingers. One touch, and the seeds would be sprouting. She couldn't let Ginger see that. "Cut it out," she said with annoyance.

Ginger looked sheepish and apologetic. "Oh, I'm sorry! I forgot about your allergy."

Jaxon struggled to regain her composure, realizing she had reacted overdramatically. Sighing, she said, "No, it's cool..." Ginger went back to watering her seeds. Jaxon tried to relax.

"So, whatever happened to your parents," Ginger pried. "Why did they give you up?"

Jaxon studied her. "Why? I think that's a little impolite to ask a foster kid, considering most of us don't really know about our parents or don't remember them. I mean, I wouldn't ask you something that personal. Who wants to remember being abandoned? Jeez, what is it with you?"

"I just wanted to know more about you, Jaxon," Ginger replied in a huff. "I don't know anyone else here, and I was trying to be your friend. But don't worry about it. I can take a hint. You've been standoffish with me ever since I got here."

Ginger's eyelids fluttered, and she looked down, trying to hide her eyes.

Jaxon felt a twinge of remorse for being harsh. She took a cautious step closer and awkwardly patted Ginger's back. "Don't do that. Don't cry. Look, I apologize. I'm distrustful by nature. It's never been my style to reveal everything about myself to a stranger. I'm not trying to be rude, I'm just..."

Ginger looked up with glistening blue eyes. "You can trust me, Jaxon. I know what it's like not to have anyone to talk to. That's been my whole life experience. But we're stuck together for the next year, at least. And just so you know, I wasn't trying to be rude by asking. I was just wondering if you'd have family or someone to come here on Saturday for the Friends and Family Day thing, cause I won't. I didn't want to have to brave it alone."

"Oh," said Jaxon, slightly embarrassed for getting upset.

Ginger flashed her a wavering smile. Jaxon thought about how crappy people had been toward her when she had first gotten to the group home, how isolated she had felt, and how she'd kept to herself to keep from getting hurt. Even though Ginger was taking a slightly different approach, coming off as invasively friendly, she had to want the same things Jaxon had wanted—to feel accepted. Jaxon decided to drop her aloofness and try to be more welcoming.

"To answer your question, I sent an invitation to my caseworker. She's the closest thing I have to family. If she comes, you can sit at the table with us. You won't have to be off to yourself." Ginger's smile grew bigger. "But Ginger, there are some things I've been meaning to talk to you about if you want us to be friends."

Ginger rocked back on her heels, her hands clasped in front of her. "Fire away. What is it?"

Jax sighed. "I can't deal with you smoking in the room. First of all, it's majorly against the rules. I hate the way it smells. The smoke gets stuck in my clothes, and it makes me cough. Can we make an agreement that you won't smoke in the room anymore?"

"Not a problem at all," Ginger replied, crossing her heart as if to signal the smoking was over.

Jaxon continued, "There's really nowhere on campus where you can get away with it. Everywhere else has cameras. If you're okay with talking to Dr. Hollis about it, maybe he can help you get on a smoking cessation program. It's a really disgusting habit anyway."

Ginger's exuberance dimmed slightly, but she didn't protest. She nodded as if she was willing to give the suggestion a try. "Anything else?" she asked.

Jaxon chose to forego her complaints about the messy room. As Otto had said, it came with the territory of having a roommate. "Just try a little harder to play by the book. You seem to be used to doing what you want to do, but I promise you'll get used to the rules around here. I did. I used to get in scuffles and brawls at every turn. I know I'm small, and you probably can't picture me fighting, but it's all I knew before I got here. At Forever Welcome, these people care about our future. If you give the place a chance, it'll change you for the better."

"Has it changed you?" Ginger asked, curious.

Jaxon smiled. "You have no idea how much... now, come on. Let's go get cleaned up so we can make it to the dining hall in time. You can sit with me and Otto again, if you want, so you don't have to eat alone."

MAY 18, 2016, AZTEC, NEW MEXICO
1:00 PM

Akiko Yamazaki tugged the wide-brimmed sunhat down to hide her face and stepped out of a rental car procured by one of Yuhle's friends. She was a few hundred miles from her government-appointed apartment in Albuquerque. Her cherry-red sundress fluttered around her slender frame as she sauntered to her destination along the dusty, almost nonexistent sidewalk. The get-up was a perfect disguise for the normally conservative woman. Oversized sunglasses covered her eyes, and platinum tresses from her blond wig floated across her golden face. She was hiding in plain sight.

In her right hand was a stamped envelope with no return address. Inside was a letter typed on an electric typewriter, the tape from the archaic machine already destroyed, leaving no trace of what was within the brief missive.

During her investigation into Gerard Terrace's information gathering with the data mining agency, Akiko had learned that technology was his access key. He could spy on any telephone or Internet traffic. He had access to public video-surveillance footage—hence her elaborate disguise—but he had no ability to trace or pore over messages sent by mail.

Akiko had worked with Yuhle to compose a warning to send to the teenage girl who, without their intervention, might soon suffer the same fate as the other Atlantis gene match subjects. As Akiko opened the glass door of the post office, she ducked her head away from the cameras, pretending to fiddle with her purse.

She walked over to the countertop, slipping into fluent Spanish. From careful research, she knew that particular post office worker would understand her. It was part of Akiko's disguise. She had studied for weeks to learn enough of the language to convincingly pull it off.

"Lo necesito para enviar una carta a mi hija en San Francisco," she said.

Akiko carried a fake ID so she could overnight the letter, and she dug it out of her handbag.

When the transaction was complete, it was all Akiko could do not to run back to the car. She continued the charade in case anyone was watching, although she knew she had covered her tracks well. There was no way Meade and his people could have followed her, but she drove to a shopping center and pretended to browse a little. She lingered in the city long enough to make sure she wasn't being tailed.

Then she drove back to the desert where her own car was waiting, shed her disguise, and drove home. She didn't dare call or text Yuhle, so she stopped by his house.

"It's done," she whispered when he opened the door. He nodded and waved her inside so they could plan their next step. They couldn't stop until they were sure the girl was safe and the Poseidon Project was shut down for good.

Chapter 13

MAY 19, 2016, SAN FRANCISCO,
CALIFORNIA
12:00 PM

Jaxon stared at the envelope in her hands as she shuffled from Dr. Hollis's office to the great room. With school officially over for the semester, many of the residents were hanging out in the spacious wood-paneled gathering spot at the front of the house. The white sofa and brown leather armchair were filled, teens sitting around the stone fireplace, others lying on the hardwood floor watching television.

Jaxon stepped into a quiet corner next to the bookshelves at the back of the room. She had never received any mail at the group home. She couldn't figure out who would need to correspond with her, and then she remembered the invitation she had sent to Helen. "Ugh. I bet she's writing back to tell me she can't make it," she mumbled.

Jax shrugged, trying not to let the prospect of spending Friends and Family Day alone faze her. She turned the envelope over to open it. "Open away from cameras" was written in small cursive letters in the back left-hand corner.

"Whatcha got?" Ginger sidled up beside her. She reached for the letter, but Jaxon pulled it back.

"I'm not sure. Dr. Hollis got this in the mail this afternoon. It was addressed to me." She swiped a finger under the seal to open the envelope, and inside was a single sheet of paper. As she read it, Jaxon's heart began to pound.

They're watching you. You're in grave danger. Whatever you do, don't let anyone else know where you're going or what you're capable of. Get to the Fourth and King Street train station by any means necessary. We will be on the lookout for you. We will find you and explain everything.

Ginger snorted over Jaxon's shoulder, having read the first few lines. "Well, that's cryptic."

Jaxon pressed the letter to her chest, glaring at her nosy roommate. "This is private, Ginger," she said.

Ginger rolled her eyes. "Looks like a chain letter," she said.

Otto ambled over and wrapped his arms around Jaxon's waist. "Just the person I wanted to see," he whispered against her cheek, kissing her face. Otto pulled away and glanced pointedly at Ginger, who reluctantly walked off to give them some privacy. "About this event tomorrow. It would be such a pleasure for me if you sit at the table with me and my parents. Loren's mom and little brother are supposed to be coming, too. We figured we'd make it a group thing, and we want to include you, my favorite group home resident." He bit his lower lip, smiling charmingly. Jaxon blushed, feeling butterflies every time she saw his handsome face, but the romantic stirrings fizzled and she came to herself, shaking the letter at Otto.

"I need you to see something," she whispered. She darted out of the great room and raced across the foyer to the kitchen to get them out of the house and away from listening ears. The patio deck that spanned the east face of the house from kitchen to dining hall was decorated with streamers and red and white balloons. The lawn was freshly cut, and a podium had been erected on the makeshift stage. A banner hanging across the entrance to the secret garden said "Welcome Friends and Family."

The staff and temp workers who had helped stage it all were now gone from the yard, the event another day off. As soon as Jaxon and Otto were alone, she shoved the letter in his hands and watched him read it. Otto's tanned face blanched, and his eyes flew to hers. "Where did this come from?" Jaxon shrugged helplessly, fearful ice-blue eyes searching his for suggestions.

"Dr. Hollis got it by mail today. How did anyone else find out about what I can do? This is serious stuff. It says someone is watching me." She felt as if she would pass out. Her breaths were coming in rapid, shallow bursts, barely enough oxygen sipped from the air. Her anxiety level skyrocketed. "What the hell is going on?" she said in a high-pitched, panicked voice.

Otto drew her into his arms and shushed her frantic thoughts. "Calm down, babe. We'll figure this out together."

"Calm down?" Jaxon pushed away from Otto's broad chest and peeked over her shoulder. "How am I supposed to do that? You saw what the letter said." Cameras were everywhere inside the house, and cameras were outside the house. There was no telling who was watching, but she could imagine how they were doing it. The letter had expressly instructed her to open it away from cameras, but she hadn't paid the note any attention. Perhaps the watchers were already aware she had found out about them. She gnawed on her bottom lip, trying to drum up a plan. She had known—she had known if anyone else found out about her powers, she would be in danger.

"I can't stay here." She shook her head, more sure of that by the second.

"You can't seriously be thinking about leaving. You know we're monitored. There's no way off the grounds without administration finding out. You won't get anywhere walking, and they'll have you back in your room before you've made it a mile down the road. There's no way you can get to that train station."

"Yeah, but what if there were some way I could leave?" Ginger, thought Jaxon. Ginger was great at getting away with breaking the rules. The innocent-looking redhead would probably jump at the opportunity to sneak her off campus. She'd also need money, and Jaxon didn't have any cash on hand, but she had a hunch Ginger would be more than happy to help her steal that, too.

"No," Otto protested, "it's too dangerous. You don't even know who you're running from, much less who you're running to!"

"I'm not going to the train station, all right? But I know I'm not safe here. All my life, I've been a survivor, a fighter. I don't sit around and wait for someone to get the best of me. I'm not about to start now."

She pushed up from the edge of the patio and dashed back into the house,

Otto close on her heels. "Don't do this," he pleaded.

Jax shook him off. He wouldn't understand. Otto was worried about Dr. Hollis and the group home administrators. Jaxon didn't have the luxury of fearing them. Regardless of who had sent the warning, the message was clear. Someone knew about her special abilities. Her life was in danger.

Jaxon found Ginger and practically dragged her out of the great room, down the hall, and up the stairs to their dorm room.

"Hey! What gives?" Ginger shook her off with a scowl.

Jaxon quickly closed and locked the door. She made a sweep of the room, looking for hidden cameras. There weren't supposed to be any in the bedrooms, but Jax had to be sure. She didn't know how to check for wires to rule them out, too, so Jaxon powered on her radio and turned up the volume loud enough to drown out their conversation.

"Ginger, I need you," she said.

Ginger instantly got serious. "What do you need? I've got you covered."

Jaxon took a deep breath, wondering if she was making the right decision. She felt as if she didn't have a choice. "I've gotta get out of here. As soon as possible. I don't know how to do that, but I'm hoping you're wily enough to lend me a hand. We haven't had time to get super close, but if you help with this, I'll be forever indebted to you. I promise you, I will not forget, and when all of this blows over, I'll repay you."

Ginger waved away the promises and launched into action. She moved over to her cluttered writing desk and yanked out the welcome folder she had been given by Dr. Hollis. There was a campus map inside. "Is this about that letter you got?" she asked, flipping through the folder. Jaxon nodded, moving closer to lean over the desk and watch. "Do you know who it was from?"

"No clue."

"Then why are you so worried?" Ginger held up the map and scanned the perimeter. "Okay, there's only officially one way onto campus and one way off, but look here. The wall that encompasses the grounds is far enough from the house, here and here, to be out of the range of any surveillance they have set up. I sincerely doubt they've wired the entire grounds. So I'm guessing if you want to make a break for it, these two spots are your best shots, but you'll have to scale the wall."

"I can do that. I'm really strong," Jaxon said absently. She turned away from Ginger and started packing a bag. She needed enough clothes to last her until she got somewhere to figure out her next move. Looking down at the duffel bag, Jaxon said reluctantly, "There's one more thing. I need money. I remember you mentioned you used to pick pockets, right?" She glanced up at Ginger, who was watching her carefully.

Ginger replied, "If you can linger around until after tomorrow's Friends and Family Day, I can get you all the money you need. But I want something from you in return."

"I told you, I'll pay you back," Jaxon said, wary. Ginger was a constantly changing creature. One minute she was bursting with excitement to help, and the next she was staring at Jaxon from her desk chair. She crossed her pale arms, and she arched a slender red brow above her cornflower-blue eyes.

"I don't need you to pay me back. I want to know why you're running. What are you hiding, Jaxon? Why would anyone be watching you?"

Jaxon shook her head. "No, I can't tell you that. I told you, I don't know who sent the letter. I don't know who's watching me."

Ginger rose with a casual shrug. "You don't know? Fine. I guess you're not hiding anything either, but that does mean I have to let Dr. Hollis know what you're up to."

"What?"

"What kind of friend would I be if I didn't? If you're in danger, he needs to know. I would've helped you run away just for kicks, but if you're running from some threat, and something happens to you while you're out there, that will be on my conscience. You can't ask me to do that. I actually like you and consider you a friend, even though I know that you're only trying to use me."

"What? No, Ginger, I've been trying to be your friend. All right, maybe I was a little bit distant at first, but that was only because I didn't understand your personality. I'm not trying to use you. I just need someone to help me do what I have to do!"

"If you're really my friend, then prove it. Show me what you're hiding," Ginger said, rising to her feet to face her.

"I'm not hiding anything!" The radio station buzzed with static at Jaxon's shout. The workbooks on her desk flew across the room like Frisbees, and the paintings on the wall started to rattle. Jax slapped a hand over her mouth in horror. Somehow, she knew she was to blame for the poltergeist activity. Her wide eyes flew to Ginger.

Ginger stared at the workbooks on the floor. She gave Jaxon a sideways glance. "Did you do that?" Jaxon shook her head. "What else can you do? The cat's out of the bag now."

Jaxon sighed, squeezing her eyes shut in defeat. She dropped her hand from her mouth and shrugged. "Lots of things, okay? I can do a lot of strange stuff. I'm learning more and more about myself with each passing day. Like, I didn't even know I could do that." She pointed to the workbooks.

Ginger squealed with delight. "Do you realize how absolutely super cool this is? This is epic. Do something else!"

Jaxon groaned, feeling like a circus performer, but did as Ginger requested, if for no other reason than to speed them along in planning her escape. Jax reached for the bed and lifted it completely off the floor with one hand. She gently set it back down. "I'm really strong, and I have a genius IQ. Happy now?"

Ginger squealed again, clapping her hands. "Oh my gosh! I can't believe you. I don't know why you'd ever worry about me telling anybody anyway. They'd all think I was off my rocker if I told them you could do that."

"Back to the matter at hand," Jaxon prompted impatiently. "The best time to get away will be while everyone is here tomorrow. Maybe right before the event is over, you and I can meet at the greenhouse, and you can hand over the money."

Ginger nodded. "That's perfect. Will you tell Otto you're leaving?"

"I can't tell anyone, least of all him. He just wouldn't understand."

"But he knows about you, right? I mean, he's your boyfriend. You probably tell him everything."

Jaxon shut her mouth, unwilling to reveal anything more about herself than she absolutely had to, and she had no desire to drag Otto into the mix. "That's not important. The important thing is that you stay in close contact with me tomorrow, which will be hard to do if you have to move through the crowd to get to... purses and all that." Jaxon was embarrassed at having to steal. It went against her principles.

"What's your cell phone number so I can text or call you when I'm ready to head to the greenhouse?" Ginger asked. Jaxon reached for the phone Ginger was handing her and keyed in her number. Ginger grinned triumphantly. "Don't worry, Jaxon. You'll be out of here soon."

MAY 19, 2016, UTAH DATA CENTER
1:00 PM

"Right there, play that back again," Gerard murmured. The tech who was looking over the group home security feeds rewound the clip and played the recording from an hour earlier. "Zoom in here. Clarify."

A small portion of the image enlarged and grew sharper with several deft, quick keystrokes, bringing the girl in the great room into focus. She was holding an envelope. When she opened it, the tech zoomed in on the message. The words were a little fuzzy, but Gerard could make out enough of the message for his lips to tighten. He swiped a hand over his bald head in frustration.

"Get General Meade on the line," he ordered. Gerard bustled from the control room to his corner office where he could talk in private. By the time he made it through the door, his assistant had already patched the general through.

Gerard sat at his oversized desk and snatched up the phone.

"What is it, Terrace?"

"Sir, we've been infiltrated. Someone's feeding the girl information about our surveillance of her. She's been instructed to leave the group home. We'll have to move fast if we want to intercept her."

"Shit!" General Meade swore. "I'll handle it. I'll take care of everything. Just keep your eyes and ears on her. If she leaves, we need to know where to start looking."

"She's a kid. There's no way she'll know how to lay low for long, and I'm not worried about that. I'm more concerned about the fact someone working on the project knew who to contact and how to contact her. Are you getting this, General? We have a rat."

The general chuckled, amused and unconcerned. "Didn't I just say I'll take care of everything? Relax, Terrace. When I make a problem disappear, it disappears completely. You have nothing to worry about, aside from keeping Jaxon Ares Andersen where you can see her. Understand?"

Gerard smiled slightly, appreciating the general's thoroughness and stoicism. "Perfectly, sir. I understand perfectly."

Chapter 14

MAY 20, 2016, SAN FRANCISCO,
CALIFORNIA

12:45 PM

Otto sat at the table with his mom and dad, but he couldn't focus on the conversation around him. Mr. and Mrs. Heike were trying to be polite to his friends, keeping up appearances, but he could tell his parents were there only to make sure he wasn't getting into trouble. Always looking for Otto to screw up, they had been amazed when he made resident assistant.

Otto's eyes roamed over the crowded backyard of Forever Welcome. The place had been transformed into a garden party with balloons tied to each chair and floral centerpieces on the tables. There was a setup for pictures and a live band performing classical music. A little fewer than a hundred people were gathered in the group home's backyard. Dr. Hollis and Mr. Vance were making their rounds, shaking hands and speaking with family members. Meanwhile, Otto could barely chew through his barbecue for worrying about Jaxon. He couldn't find her.

The Friends and Family Day had kicked off with an awards ceremony for the residents, followed by lively games and outdoor sports. Jaxon had made her way to his side earlier in the day to meet his parents, but when folks settled down to eat, she had disappeared. He knew she was supposed to be sharing a table with her caseworker and Ginger, but neither of the girls were in sight, although earlier he had seen Ginger darting around from table to table.

Loren leaned over and whispered furtively, "I don't see her either." He hadn't told Loren about Jaxon's plan to run away, but he had asked his fellow resident assistant to keep an eye on her. Loren pushed her wheat-blond bangs out of her face and shrugged. "She'll show up eventually."

Otto's instincts were telling him something was wrong. He whispered back, "Keep the folks entertained. I'll be back. I need to make sure she's all right." Loren gave him a solemn nod. As Otto excused himself to go to the restroom, Lo directed the attention of her mom and his parents to the patio, where artwork was on display. Otto flashed Loren a thumbs-up and disappeared into the crowd.

Jaxon pushed through the garden and rushed over to the greenhouse. She had gotten a text message from Ginger stating the "work" was done and to meet her there, but when she opened the frosted glass door and peered inside, the stifling hot room was empty. Nothing was inside but rows of plants, mulch on the ground, and a table in the middle of the floor still littered with potting soil from Ginger's plantings days. Jaxon bit back an expletive and parked her hip against the side of the table to wait for her friend to arrive, hoping Ginger hadn't gotten caught.

"This was so stupid," she groaned, putting her face in her palm and thinking of how much trouble they could get into. "I never should have dragged her into this." Jax clutched her temples and massaged. She had spent the day watching happy families reunite, siblings hang out together, and moms and dads show pride in their wayward children's rehabilitation. Though Helen had shown up to see Jax receive her award for highest GPA, the caseworker had to leave early, which was fine by Jaxon. She preferred Helen not be present for the prison break. She wanted to save the kindly caseworker some embarrassment.

Everything had seemed as if it was going according to plan. Ginger had been a social butterfly, flitting from table to table and meeting and charming folks with her artless knack for being engaging. Jaxon had barely noticed her reaching surreptitiously into purses and back pockets—and she knew that the girl was stealing. Jax could only imagine how surprised the victims would be when they got home and realized their wallets had been emptied. No one noticed they were being robbed.

Now, it was time for her to get the money and make a run for it. The Friends and Family Day celebration would be over in a few hours. If she didn't make a break for it, she'd miss her window of opportunity. Jaxon had already stowed the duffel bag with her belongings under the center table. She knew Dr. Hollis wouldn't have time to review the surveillance footage before the party was over, and she would be long gone by then. She was all set to flee to the far wall surrounding the property and climb to her freedom, but where was Ginger?

There was a tap on the greenhouse door. Jaxon spun around, her hopes dashed when it wasn't her roommate. A frisson of nervousness zinged through her when her boyfriend walked through the door and stared at her with a suspicious squint. "What are you doing here?" she asked breathlessly. Her eyes shifted guiltily. She had regretted slipping away without saying good-bye to him, but Jaxon had planned on calling him after she cleared the grounds. Just her luck, she was running behind, giving Otto the opportunity to come look for her. If he found out what she was trying to do, she knew it was the resident assistant's job to tell on her.

He stepped closer with a soft scowl. "I should be asking you that. What are *you* doing in here? I've been looking for you everywhere. Loren noticed your caseworker leaving and figured you'd be lonesome by yourself, but then I lost track of you. Are you all right?"

"Huh? Yeah. No, I'm fine," she said too brightly. Jaxon bit her tongue and glanced away, hating to lie to him. "I came out here to get some alone time. You know how much I hate crowds. Everything should be over soon anyway, right? Why don't you go back out and enjoy your family?"

Otto eyed her curiously. "Well, I kind of wanted to include—"

Jaxon yelped in surprise as the greenhouse door flew open. A small stone hurled through the air, glass shattering and knocking the surveillance camera out of commission. Jaxon's heart dropped to her feet. Otto swore soundly and threw Jax behind his back when three burly men in military fatigues burst into the small, cramped space. "Stay back, Otto! I've got this," she yelled, instinctively placing herself in front of Otto, gearing up for a fight. Her forceful shove sent him skidding behind her and into a corner.

Jaxon dropped low and sprang into the air, landing in the center of the greenhouse table with a light thud. She kicked down ceramic flowerpots and planters that clattered into one another and crashed to the floor. She pivoted three hundred and sixty degrees, quickly examining each of her opponents with flinty blue eyes. Her fists were raised and her feet slightly spread, in position to take on all three men. She didn't know who they were, but she had a good idea of why they were there. They were sent by "them," the watchers. Guns were pointed at her torso, and she quickly determined they were tranquilizer guns. Of course—the enemy would want her alive. What use were her abilities if she was dead?

Jax stamped down on the gun nearest her hard enough to render it unusable, simultaneously crouching and turning to snatch the weapon from the man to her left and use it to bash the man to her right in the face. His head snapped back, and he cried out. Jax broke the gun she was holding in half. It all happened so rapidly that Otto thought she moved in a blur. The men weren't out for the count, however. Martial arts training was apparent when a nimble soldier sprang up on the table behind her.

"Jax, look out!" Otto shouted.

She spun clockwise with her right leg high in the air, bringing her foot to the attacker's face to steady it for her spin kick with the left leg. She punched with both fists, slamming into the man's chest and throat, sending him flying. The attacker she had smashed in the face with a gun grabbed her leg and yanked her off balance. Jaxon hit the table with a painful *thwack*, and she scrambled backward, pushing off the edge of the table to throw her body upright.

Otto launched up from the ground, grabbing a handful of mulch that he flung into one assailant's eyes, sending the injured soldier reeling back with an angry shout. The man Jax had sent flying into the greenhouse wall was groggily trying to stand, and an uninjured soldier sped forward. She swept aside the man's punches, blocking kicks and jabbing out with her elbow to clip him in the nose. He reached for another weapon from the holster at his waist, and she brought her hands together in a mighty fist that crunched down on his collar bone. The man screamed and dropped to his knees.

Jaxon jerked around to help Otto, who was going hand to hand with the soldier that had brought her down. She grabbed the man around the upper torso, lifting him and throwing his body down with enough force to stun him.

When all the soldiers were disabled, Jaxon grabbed Otto's hand and shot out of the greenhouse. They fled through the garden, Jaxon looking wildly over her shoulders to make sure they weren't being followed. Her breath whooshed from her lungs, and her heartbeat thundered in her chest like a runaway train. Perspiration flew off her body like raindrops. She kept running.

Sliding through the archway where the purple wisteria drifted down like raindrops, Jaxon looked up with wide, fearful eyes as it seemed everyone at the party turned their attention to her grand reentrance. She skated to a halt, and Otto crashed into her, both of them going down. Startled guests of the Friends and Family Day circled around the fallen couple, and Dr. Hollis muscled through the crowd to see what was going on.

"She's hurt!" someone shouted in alarm. Jax suddenly realized she was bleeding. A gash in her chin from where she had fallen on the table in the greenhouse trickled crimson down her neck. She threw her hand to the wound to stanch the flow.

"Get back! Everyone get back!" Anthony ordered.

Mr. Vance dashed up to the podium and called for calm. With hands raised, he directed everyone to look at him. "I'm going to have to ask our residents, guests, and non-essential staff to return to the main building. Please don't run. Let's all walk in an orderly fashion. There is no cause for panic. The situation is being assessed. Essential staff members, please direct traffic. Let's stay calm, everybody." He beckoned for the rest of his staff, decked out in crisp gray uniforms, to assist with moving the crowd indoors.

Jaxon shakily sat up, and Otto rose to his feet. His parents rushed to his side. Dr. Hollis knelt over Jaxon. "What happened to you? Are you all right? Who did this?" Dr. Hollis fired questions. Jax shrugged, shaking her head. She didn't know how to explain that people were after her—or why.

"Sir, some men somehow got onto the grounds and attacked her in the greenhouse. If I hadn't been there, they might have hurt her worse," Otto blurted. Mrs. Heike gasped in shock at the news that her son had been present during an attack of some sort. Jaxon glared at Otto, hurt by his betrayal of her secret that she was being pursued, but Otto didn't feel he had a choice. Men had broken onto campus to harm her, and there was no way he could stand by and keep mum. Others might try to attack her again. He couldn't let that happen.

Anthony's eyebrows shot up, and his mouth dropped open. "What do you mean, someone attacked Jax? Who would do something like that?" It was Friends and Family Day, but not just any and every guest was allowed on campus. If an invitee had a felony or past history of crime, he didn't make the cut. Why would anyone from the mix of parents, siblings, and family friends try to harm Jaxon Andersen?

"What on earth are you talking about, Otto?" asked Mr. Heike. He clutched his son by the shoulders and quickly looked him over for injuries, not finding any but upset nonetheless that Otto could have been hurt. "Dr. Hollis? What's the meaning of this? This is supposed to be a safe school, or so say all the brochures. What kind of place are you running?"

"How could you let something like this happen?" Mrs. Heike asked.

Mr. Vance hurried over at the tail end of the parents' questions after getting the rest of the guests headed inside. "What's going on, Anthony?" Mr. Vance fixed him with a demanding stare as if the psychiatrist had some explaining to do. Anthony was in charge of the residents, but it seemed unsupportive to him that even the administrator of the group home was looking at him as if he had done something wrong.

"Th-they said someone attacked them at the greenhouse," Anthony stammered. He didn't know what to say to that or whether to believe it. It sounded ludicrous that anyone would scale the wall to get inside and try to hurt his residents. The wall was mostly ornamental. The group home was isolated enough that they didn't have to worry about crime, other than from the juveniles housed at the facility. All of them had records. He stared at Jaxon and Otto suspiciously. "Are you guys sure that's what happened?"

Mr. Vance's gaze flew to the archway that led to the gardens. "Do you smell that? I smell smoke," he said, hurrying off in the direction of the acrid scent, and Anthony and the Heikes followed quickly.

Otto helped Jaxon to her feet. She tried to pull away, but he tightened his grip and stared at her. "I can't let anything happen to you," he whispered fiercely.

"Otto, I love you," Jaxon said. She caught herself, realizing what she had said. His stormy eyes softened. His tense lips parted slightly, and he drew her into a brief, tender kiss. Jaxon pushed out of his arms with a shake of her head. "No, you don't understand. I love you, but I have to leave you. Don't you see? If you stay with me, the same people after me have no qualms about hurting you. It's dangerous, Otto. I was already making plans to get out of this place later tonight, but now that you told everyone about the men at the greenhouse, they'll be watching the entire wall." She turned away from him, feeling hopeless. She had to figure out a new way to leave. Dr. Hollis, Mr. Vance—no one there could save her from the people who were after her, not even Otto.

Mr. Vance and Dr. Hollis came running back through the archway, Otto's parents in their wake. Mr. Vance was speaking animatedly into his cell phone. "Yes, 9-1-1! We need emergency responders to Forever Welcome group home immediately!" He ran toward the house with the phone pressed to his ear. Mrs. Heike marched over to Otto and threw back her arm, slapping him squarely in the face. His head whipped aside. Otto slowly turned back to his mother and stared at her in shock.

"How could you?" she yelled. "After everything we've done to get you off the hook for that crap you pulled with Benson's barn? We don't have the money to keep fixing your stupid mistakes! We sent you here to get help!" Her words trailed off to sobs, and Mr. Heike tucked his wife in his arms and pulled her away. Jaxon jumped to Otto's defense, putting herself between him and his parents.

"Mom, what did I do?" Otto asked.

Mr. Heike looked at him with disappointment. "Just stop it, buddy, okay? Look, I'll get our lawyer on the phone and see what he can do, but you might have to sit a spell for this one. I've got to get your mom home."

Otto stood there with a confused expression, holding his stinging face as his parents turned their backs on him and shuffled away.

Dr. Hollis inhaled shakily and looked depressed as he gestured back through the arch, eyes boring into his resident assistant. "Otto, I'm afraid you'll need to pack your bags. Your probation officer is being contacted. You'll be leaving the group home immediately."

Jaxon stared at Dr. Hollis, dumbfounded. "Why? Why are you doing this?" Suddenly, she smelled it, too. Smoke. Jax shielded her eyes and looked up. Beyond the stone wall that separated the backyard from the garden, clouds of thick black smoke poured into the clean blue sky. She gripped Otto's hand and asked fearfully, "What about the men who attacked us?"

Dr. Hollis glared at her coldly. "Jaxon, there were no men. But we did find accelerants and a raging fire that will likely spread far beyond the greenhouse before the fire department gets here, and that's going to cost thousands—probably tens of thousands—of dollars to repair! There's only one person out here who has a history of starting fires like that."

"But he didn't do anything. I was there. Neither of us did anything wrong!"

"First of all, you were supposed to be in the backyard with the rest of the residents and enjoying the festivities. Consider your points docked for leaving without permission. Now maybe you thought if you made up some story about intruders, then you could help him get off the hook, but just tell me, kids, who were these mystery men, and why would they be after you, Jaxon?"

"Because... because." She faltered. Jax couldn't tell Dr. Hollis, even to get Otto out of trouble.

Otto grabbed her hand and squeezed. "It's okay."

"I can't believe you two would stoop to this level of debauchery on a day like this while we have guests visiting the residence. Not only have you made yourselves look bad, but also your behavior reflects on the school, and you've put my career on the line. Did you stop to think about that while you were out setting fires and what have you? And lying to cover for your boyfriend isn't helping him or you. You're both in trouble. Now, get back to the house until I can speak with you in private."

Jaxon stumbled back, stung by his harshness. Dr. Hollis had never spoken to her like that before. Worse, everyone was under the impression Otto had started the fire. "Are you kidding me?" she shouted. Dr. Hollis jabbed a finger in the direction of the house. She spun away from the psychiatrist, blinded by tears. There was nothing she could say or do to help the situation.

Otto had tried telling the truth so the people who were supposed to protect the residents could do their damn jobs, but Dr. Hollis and Mr. Vance didn't believe him. Thanks to Jaxon, Otto would be carted off like a common criminal and likely charged with arson. Sobs tore from her chest as she kept walking. She couldn't look back. She didn't want to see the look on Otto's face, that despairing look that said everything he had worked so hard for was being taken away, and it was all her fault.

Mr. Vance rushed past her. "The fire truck's out front. They're coming now. Get that student to your office, Hollis! You'll be in the way out here."

Jaxon crashed through the kitchen door and ran past the people congregated in the foyer and great room. She sprinted to the stairs and flew up to her bedroom. When she swung open the door, there was Ginger, sitting on the bed and looking out the window at Dr. Hollis angrily leading Otto into the house. The beautiful lawn was quickly trampled by firefighters, hoses crisscrossing through the grass. They filed through the archway to the gardens to put out the fire, which could be seen easily from the upstairs bedroom, and Jaxon pressed her face to the glass. The flames had leapt from the greenhouse to the orchards, and the fire was swiftly consuming all it could.

She wondered what had happened to the men that attacked her. They had to be gone by then. But how had they known she would be at the greenhouse? Even if the watchers had her under surveillance, she had cobbled together the plan to flee only the night before. Jaxon hadn't been near any of the surveillance cameras; she had made sure the room was clear before recruiting Ginger to help her escape, and she hadn't told anyone else about what they were planning to do. No one knew but her roommate. She turned from the window and glared at Ginger. "You," Jaxon growled. "You led me to the greenhouse to be ambushed!"

"What? How could I—"

"You sent me that text message telling me to meet you there, but you never showed up. Is that a coincidence, Ginger?" Jaxon menacingly advanced on the girl. Ginger shrank into herself, trying to explain.

"No, I got to the garden and saw those people in camouflage lurking around and knew they were sent by whoever is after you. I tried to warn you! I sent you a second text message telling you to steer clear of the greenhouse and meet me up here in the room, but then I saw you headed to the greenhouse anyway. Didn't you get my text?"

Jaxon jerked her smartphone out of her back pocket and flashed it in Ginger's face. "No missing texts, you liar. You set me up!" She grabbed Ginger around the neck and squeezed, shaking her. Ginger's eyes widened, and she coughed, sputtering. She flailed for her cell phone, knocking it off the nightstand onto the floor.

"Jaxon, stop. Please! Why would I set you up? I'm not the enemy here. We're in this together. Just check my phone. You'll see I sent you the message." Jaxon released the pleading girl and angrily snatched up Ginger's cellphone.

Jax scrolled through the messages and stared down at the two most recent ones, the only two sent to her phone number. The first message was the one she had received, telling her to meet Ginger at the greenhouse. The second message was in all caps, a texted scream—DON'T GO TO THE GH! COME TO OUR ROOM! MEN WITH GUNS!

Jax sank to the floor by Ginger's bed and shook her head at the irony of missing the more important text. Anything could have caused her not to get the message—a lost signal, a delay in reception. Either way, Otto was in trouble, the greenhouse was destroyed, and her chances of getting off campus were slim to none. Oh, and she had just tried to kill the one person who was trying to help her out of the whole mess.

"I'm sorry, Ginger." Jaxon's shoulders slumped, her head bowing. She was close to giving up. Hot tears arced down her cheeks, but she dashed them away with her fists. Crying never solved anything. She had to think.

Ginger sighed, rubbing her neck. "Anyway, I got the money," she mumbled tersely. She shook wads of crumpled bills from inside her pillowcase and counted the cash on her bed, four hundred dollars in total. "I don't know if that'll be enough, but it's a start. Still leaving tonight?"

Jaxon bit back a sob. "Dr. Hollis will be watching everything I do from now on, especially tonight. Those men you saw lurking near the greenhouse ended up attacking me and Otto. I managed to take the three men down, but they set fire to the greenhouse. Now Dr. Hollis thinks we made up the story about being attacked to cover for Otto. He thinks Otto set the fire."

"That sucks, totally," said Ginger. "Thank goodness I always operate with a plan B in the wings. I just happened to call in a favor from my caseworker while I was waiting up here for you, just in case something went wrong with the runaway."

"You what?" Jaxon folded the money and placed it under her mattress. Sliding down to sit on the floor in the space between their twin beds, she looked at Ginger. Wispy tendrils of red hair hung around the girl's freckled face. Ginger's strawberry-red lips curled upward slightly in a mischievous smile, and Jax got nervous. "Please don't tell me you told someone else about me. I really can't take any more bad news right now. I'm already freaking out about what might happen to Otto."

Ginger shook her head. "Nothing of any consequence, at least. I informed my caseworker that you're in need of a safe, discreet placement. He's got connections like you wouldn't believe."

"Yeah, but he's *your* caseworker. How the heck is that supposed to help me?" Jaxon said. She dropped her head back on the side of her bed and stared at the ceiling.

Ginger clambered down to sit next to her, whispering conspiratorially. "After meeting your caseworker, I mentioned her to my caseworker. Jaxon, everything is being worked out in your favor. He's pulling some strings to get you released from the group home early, making you eligible to be taken into another foster home, and he says he knows just the family for you. I told him to make shit happen pronto, and I hope you don't mind, but I hinted that you were being victimized by a guy here and were too scared to talk to the administrators. So, he assured me he can have the family out here to pick you up no later than next week, and none of the administrators here have to know anything about it."

None of it made sense. Jaxon was very familiar with the foster care system. She had been a part of it all her life. Nothing ever happened that quickly. Jaxon looked at Ginger uncertainly. "But if you thought I was running away, why would you tell your caseworker about me?"

"Just trust me," Ginger murmured, sliding her hand on top of Jaxon's. "I get feelings, Jax. I had a feeling today would end badly, but whoever those goons were, they're not going to try to get in the same way again. They'll wait awhile before they make another attack, which gives you time to get away while they're plotting the next coup. I'm sure you caught 'em off guard today. They had to set the fire to cover their tracks."

Jaxon groaned. "Or they know Otto's history with fires and figured they could get him out of the picture now. After all, they're watching me... oh, my God. Ginger, you might be in danger, too!"

Ginger snorted. "Darling, I grew up in the crummiest hovels you could call home. I can do far worse things to someone who tries to hurt me than you could ever imagine. Don't worry on my account," she said. Jaxon trembled at the bite in Ginger's voice, believing her for some reason. "At any rate, you've gotta stop worrying about the people around you and take better care of yourself. They don't want us... they want you."

Chapter 15

MAY 23, 2016, ALBUQUERQUE, NEW
MEXICO

1:50 AM

Akiko opened her eyes. The sound of her
raspy, labored breathing had awakened
her. She was in a dimly lit room, squares
overhead illuminated by soft white, the
light not strong enough to banish the
darkness. The round lamps attached
to the ceiling by double-jointed metallic
arms weren't powered on. She recognized
the examination room lamps, vaguely.
Akiko's dark brown eyes rolled sluggish-

ly to the right and fluttered weakly to the left. Yes, some sort of examination room. She tried to swallow because her throat was dry, but her tongue felt heavy and uncooperative in her mouth.

The last thing Akiko remembered was climbing into her king-sized bed at her apartment. She wasn't in her bed, though. Her weighted arms were tucked against her body atop what felt like a cool leather reclining chair. Her fingers tingled when she tried to flex her hand.

The walls of the room were painted dense black, which seemed odd to Akiko. She tried to laugh at the absurd color scheme, but it came out sounding like air deflating from a balloon. Then again, she realized, the walls weren't painted black. They were glass. The room was surrounded with windows. Her skittish breath hitched on the inhale. She recognized the place. It was the basement examination room at Starke, the Poseidon Project's main staging area.

"Glad you could join us, Dr. Yamazaki," said General Meade.

She tried to turn her head, but she was restrained. Someone was in the room with her—several people, actually.

Akiko heard soft whispers and the beep of a monitor. She was wired to a Holter for her heart, an electroencephalogram for her brain. She was pricked by an IV attached to a drip. Akiko tried to protest, but whatever drug they had used to bring her there was still potent enough to make her words slur. "Whaaa yew doing meee…"

General Meade stepped forward out of the shadows into the cool spill of weak light. "Now, shouldn't I be asking you that?" he said with a sinister smile. "Shouldn't I be asking, Dr. Yamazaki, why are you doing this to me?" He held up a copy of the letter she had sent to Jaxon Andersen.

Akiko exhaled a long, slow sigh. They were going to kill her. They had probably gotten Yuhle, too. Worse, their deaths would be in vain. With no one there to help the girl escape, General Meade—with the rest of those in the Poseidon Project—would soon have Jaxon in their grasp to do the unspeakable things they had done to the others with the Atlantis gene.

"Y-y-yew neeed"—she struggled to form the words—"need me."

"I did," General Meade allowed. He paced around the bed in the center of the main examination room. Countless other subjects had lain in that same bed. They had been drugged until docile and forced to show off their inhuman abilities. Meade had seen their strengths and their weaknesses, and the Atlantis descendants were now serving a higher purpose. They were arrested in suspended animation. They would barely age and never get sick. They wouldn't die—until Meade decided to pull the plugs. The test subjects were being cultivated and harvested so their DNA could be spliced with other modified human DNA to create an advanced special force.

When the aliens returned—and they would, soon—America wouldn't be caught with the proverbial pants down. Thanks to General Meade, the country would be prepared to launch a preemptive strike. The modified hybrids created by the Poseidon Project would be better suited to fight the alien tide, and they were expendable. Meade simply needed a prototype to prove the hybrids' worth to the powers that were who were dragging their feet on okaying the genetic manipulations—manipulations they were unaware were already taking place. He needed Jaxon Andersen to remold, train, and turn into the ultimate agent to show the bureaucrats the project wasn't a waste of time and money. If Meade could have her, then the rest was history.

But the geneticist had underhandedly tried to deter him from that mission. Meade tsked sadly. "I did need you," he murmured. "Unfortunately for you, I don't anymore. You see, Dr. Yamazaki, I've found someone else who can do what you do, and he understands the gravity and scope of the threat against us. Of course, I had hoped it wouldn't come to this. Back when you started lying about the test results, I knew you couldn't be trusted, but to go behind my back and do this?" He shook the letter.

Akiko strained against her restraints, growing stronger. "You d-don't have the Mother copy," she countered. Without a sample for comparison, finding the Atlantis gene matches would be a shot in the dark. They'd probably hit upon some lucky breaks by comparing with the new samples, but the DNA from the current test subjects was much more muddled with the human genome. It would take ages.

"I thought you'd say that," said Meade.

He pressed a button on the remote hidden in his pocket. A holographic screen appeared in front of Dr. Yamazaki. On the screen was the copy of the Mother gene. She swallowed a sob. They had stolen it from her. She didn't know how. The copy had been on her personal computer, secured by encryptions and a bevy of passwords. General Meade had dashed her last hope of getting out alive, and she was truly replaceable.

Akiko found herself laughing, soft chuckles that grew in volume to gasping croaks. She jerked against the restraints again. The drug had almost worn off completely. "You can kill me, Meade... but you won't get away with it... My w-work is my legacy. The scientific community will rise up against you to see... to see to it that you are punished for what you think you do in the dark. You think no one will ask? No one will wonder what happened to me?"

Meade calmly clasped his hands behind his back and stared down at her with a pitying look. "Dear, when I make a problem disappear, it disappears. You have no legacy. All your prior work is being discredited as we speak. Word is being disseminated that you copied from other researchers, forged test results, and cheated on peer reviews. By the time they put you in the ground, you'll be the laughing stock of genetics."

She cried out, "No! You can't do that to me!"

"It's already been done." He leaned forward, taking delicious pleasure in the tears that sprang to her eyes. "But I'm not going to kill you, Akiko. That would be too easy, too predictable."

He beckoned for the doctor waiting in the shadows to step forward. The furtive little man darted to Akiko's side and placed a syringe into the medication port of her IV. She tried to resist, but whatever he had given her acted fast.

Meade said, "I'm not going to kill you because I want you to suffer what you tried to do to me, ungrateful little meddler. I want you to feel what it's like to be so close to something you really want only to have someone try to come along and take it away from you. See, you tried to put me in an awkward position here. Can you blame me? So now, whenever you talk, people will look at you like you're talking gibberish. How are you feeling, Akiko?" He chuckled, a deep rumble.

She writhed on the examination bed. Akiko felt sharp tingles shooting up and down her right arm and leg until the limbs dragged against the rest of her body like deadweights. The right side of her face twisted, sinking lower than the left. Her right visual cortex lost signals. The cries that sprang from her tingling lips were incoherent.

Even as the stroke continued to ravage her brain, General Meade continued with the rest of his dark plan. He had her removed from the examination bed and carted to her laboratory. She was gingerly placed on the floor. If anyone questioned what had happened to her, it would look as if the doctor had suffered a brain aneurysm while working. When the setup was complete, Meade strutted to the elevators, his new right-hand man at his side.

"I think you're going to like working here, Dr. Jones. And don't worry about Dr. Yamazaki back there. Our medical insurance is top of the line."

"Oh, I'm sure I will, Meade. I'm sure I will."

Epilogue

MAY 30, 2016, ALBUQUERQUE, NEW
MEXICO

8:00 PM

Yuhle walked into the ICU at Presbyterian Hospital where his boss and mentor was convalescing from the disabling stroke that had left her face and body twisted, her mind unable to function. Dr. Yamazaki was a fairly young woman, in her late thirties. Her physicians couldn't seem to find a reason for the severity of her stroke, much less why she had had one so early in life. But in a lot of ways, the malady seemed a blessing in disguise. With Dr. Yamazaki out of commission, General Meade and the Poseidon Project didn't seem to need Yuhle. He had broken ties with them.

Yuhle pushed his ever-slipping and sliding glasses up the bridge of his nose and smiled down at Akiko, who was awake and staring at him with her good eye. She couldn't talk, but she could understand him. He leaned down and whispered in her ear out of habit. He would never again take privacy for granted. Ever since working on the project, Yuhle was much more aware of unwanted eyes and ears.

"I've assembled the team you started putting together before you had the... accident... the ones who will help us find the rest of the Atlantis descendants and rescue them from Meade," he whispered. "They gave me a message to report back to you. They're going after the girl. Meade won't rest until he has her in his grasp."

"Mehhhh," Akiko groaned.

Yuhle nodded encouragingly. "That's right, Doctor. He'll have to get through us first. The Atlantis Allegiance is in place."

About the Author

S.A. Beck lives in sunny California. When she's not surfing, knitting or daydreaming in a hammock, she's writing novels.

19214421R00170

Printed in Great Britain
by Amazon